FRIENDLY PERSUASION . . .

"You should know something, stranger," the man said quickly. "Fairoaks is a nice town filled with nice folks. If there was any doubt in a single mind, this terrible thing would not be done."

Somebody cracked a hand on the flank of the horse and it lunged forward with a snort of complaint. The men holding the rope tightened their grip and tensed their muscles to take the strain.

"No!" Emmet Ford screamed, then was silent except for the crack of his breaking neck as his body fell free and was pulled up short. His body shook in spasms and was then limp. His head hung at an unnatural angle as the whole dead weight swayed gently.

A couple of men smiled but the rest remained grim-faced. One groaned, but, whether from relief or remorse, it was impossible to judge.

"Sorry you had to see that," Wallace muttered to Steele. "This ain't the kinda impression of Fairoaks people we want strangers to get. On account of it ain't a true one."

ADAM STEELE SERIES:

No. 11
George G. Gilman

ADAM **STEELE**

LYNCH TOWN

PINNACLE BOOKS • LOS ANGELES

ADAM STEELE #11: LYNCH TOWN

Copyright © 1976 by George G. Gilman

First American edition.
First published in Great Britain by
New English Library Limited.

A Pinnacle Books edition, published by special arrangement with New English Library Limited.
First printing, October 1978

ISBN: 0-523-40370-4

Cover illustration by Fred Love

Printed in the United States of America

PINNACLE BOOKS, INC.
2029 Century Park East
Los Angeles, California 90067

for:
Molly and Brian
an ill-matched pair
according to the stars

LYNCH TOWN

CHAPTER ONE

The boy was close to anguished exhaustion as he staggered through the redwood forest, the breath rattling in his nostrils and rasping through his clenched teeth. Although the rich foliage of the giant trees filtered much of the intense heat from the mid-afternoon sunlight, heavy sweat squeezed out of wide-open pores to course across exposed skin, and more salty moisture pasted the white cotton shirt and Levis to his body and limbs.

Sweat and tears blurred his vision and muscle cramps attacked his legs. He fell often, tripping on low brush or crashing into the massive trunks of the towering trees. But, although he veered constantly to left and right, never seeing a single detail of his thickly timbered surroundings clearly, the instinct for self-preservation kept him headed in a southwesterly direction.

He was about eighteen, close to six feet tall and with a lean build, a handsome boy with clean-cut features beneath a mop of thick, short-clipped black hair. But there was inevitably a quality of ugliness overlaid on his basic good looks now, as he made his gasping, sobbing, staggering run through the timber country of northern California in the broad valley between the Sierra

1

Nevadas and the Coast Range of mountains. An ugliness that glowed in his squinting green eyes and emanated from the strange twist to his ever-moving mouthline; caused mainly by the agony of driving his tortured body so hard but derived also from the stark terror that had created torment in his mind even before the desperate race for his life had begun.

Then, as he slammed into a trunk and the additional impetus of the collision sent him reeling out into a grassy clearing, a cry of pain was curtailed to give vent to a yell of delight. Until he emerged into the sun-bright opening among the trees, he had trusted his instincts to hold him on a course away from deadly pursuit. Now, as he came to a panting, swaying halt and wiped the sweat and tears from his eyes, he was exhilarated to discover his innate sense for survival had proved itself once again.

The clearing had always been a favorite place for him in less troubled times; today its importance was vital. For in the shade at the western side was a small pool of crystal clear water fed by an underground spring. Often in the past, when he had come here simply to be alone, he had drunk from the pool, but never had he needed the refreshing and sustaining effects of the cool water more urgently than today.

He did not drink recklessly though, and after lowering his tortured body onto the grass and dipping his burning face into the pool, he drank slowly to avoid choking and stomach cramps; and he did not allow the luxury of rest and refreshment to undermine his alertness. He continued to listen intently for the slightest sound that might mean his pursuers were drawing close.

He remained in the prone position for a full thirty seconds, alternately sucking at the water and breathing deeply. During this time, the only other sounds he heard were from the wildlife in the surrounding timber: the calls of quails and pigeons, the tapping of a woodpecker and the rustling of brush as small animals crisscrossed the forest.

Then he heard an alien noise.

He rolled suddenly onto his back, fear taking command of his face to the exclusion of exhaustion. And he held his breath as he snatched a Manhattan Navy Colt from his belt. He had identified the sound the moment he heard it—the shod hooves of a horse moving slowly through the brush. As he lay on his back, fresh sweat oozing to join the beads of water clinging to his light bristles, he took a bearing on the direction from which the horse was approaching.

And there was no consolation in the fact that the rider was nearing the clearing from the southeast. Nor that he was whistling softly and tunefully—obviously unaware that on this hot afternoon this patch of country was host to latent violence, set to explode into reality by the merest touch against a feather-light trigger. For, although the boy's pursuers were coming from the northeast, discovery by anybody from any direction could prove ultimately fatal. Unless . . .

The boy showed his teeth in a thin smile as he rolled onto his belly again and sprang erect. The possibility of obtaining a horse turned the prospect of being discovered from misfortune into hope for a better chance of survival.

He moved quickly and silently into the cover of a California oak, which stood on the edge of the pool.

Adam Steele did not sense the presence of the boy until his gray gelding smelt water and snorted eagerness to drink. Of its own volition, the horse lengthened its stride as it achieved the side of the clearing, but immediately responded to the command of the reins and reduced the pace to what it had been before.

The boy had caught a brief glimpse of the newcomer and gelding, before he drew his head sharply back into the solid cover of the oak.

The man he saw was in the early thirties, short and built on lean lines. No taller than five feet six or seven with a body that suggested compact strength rather than slightness. His manner of dress was basically city-style—a gray suit, claret-colored vest, white shirt and black shoelace tie. But, set squarely on his head was a black Stetson; the spurless boots he wore under the cuffs of his pants were ideal footwear for riding; and there was a gray kerchief hanging loosely around his neck.

He therefore looked something of a dude—the kerchief the only item of his apparel showing signs of long and hard wear—but a dude prepared to adapt his style to the needs of his mode of travel and the country he traveled.

Because the sun was midway into its slide down the western side of the sky, his hat brim did not shade his face. It was a pleasant face with a kind of nondescript handsomeness in the set of the regular features. The skin was burnished by long exposure to the sun, and carved with many lines which cut away from either side of the coal black eyes and the gentle mouthline. There was little of his neatly clipped hair to be seen below the hat brim, except that which formed his long sideburns, and this was mostly gray, with just a trace of red showing here and there.

The saddle on the gelding was fairly new and well cared for, fitted with a rifle boot, canteen, twin bags and a lariat. Lashed to the bedroll was a stained and torn sheepskin coat.

The man wore no gunbelt and the only weapon in full view was a Colt Hartford revolving rifle with its stock jutting from the boot. The boy did not see the split in the seam of the man's right pants leg, so had no reason to suspect that this gave access to a knife located in a boot sheath. Neither did he notice that the kerchief was weighted at diagonally opposite corners, to make it into an unorthodox but nonetheless deadly weapon. And the ornate stickpin, which Steele had used to good effect on a number of occasions, was completely hidden—behind the lapel of the sheepskin coat.

Both rider and horse showed just a few signs of weariness. The gelding was anxious to drink and the man's jaw was bristled. Dust clung to dried sweat on the flanks of the animal and the rider's face was sheened, streaked here and there with dirt from where he had run a hand across his moist flesh. It was obvious they had traveled far, but without haste.

In fact, Steele felt pleasantly lethargic and had been looking for just such a place as this to rest for a while and boil up some coffee. But his drowsiness caused by heat and travel evaporated like a drip of water on a red hot stove lid the instant his horse took long strides into the clearing and he sensed he was not alone.

But, even had the boy risked a longer look, he would have seen no visible reaction to hint at Steele's change of mood. For the Virginian's mind became intently alert without altering his impassive expression by a flicker, and he tensed his muscles for sudden action while maintaining his casual posture astride the gelding. His gaze shifted from one point in the clearing to another with no outward sign that he was anything more than idly curious about his new surroundings.

But there was nothing to see except the ring of trees, expanse of lush grass and the clear pool of water in shade. And the Virginian's straining ears heard only the sounds of nature which had been more or less the same since he came down from the Sierras and rode into the forest cloaking the foothills and filling this part of the valley.

He nonetheless trusted the feeling of being watched as he kept the gelding on a tight rein and rode slowly toward the pool. By how many pairs of eyes he was not prepared to guess, but he was certain the eyes were hostile.

"Freeze, mister!"

The boy stepped out from behind the big oak on the far side of the pool, the Colt held in a double-handed grip and pushed forward to the full stretch of his long arms. His sweating face above the vee of his arms was set in an expression of grim intent and his hands were rock steady to aim the gun at Steele's chest.

6

The Virginian's eyelids did not flicker as the boy appeared. The horse had reached the bank of the pool and lowered its head to drink. Steele had slid his left foot out of the stirrup and moved his hands slowly, one to fist around the saddle horn and the other close to the jutting stock of the Colt Hartford.

And it was in this attitude that he complied with the order, setting no store by the youth of the gunman, but reading from the boy's expression that he was ready to shoot and knowing from the steadiness of the aim that he would hit the target.

"I don't wanna kill you, mister. But I sure will if I have to."

"I believe you, son," Steele drawled, his accent revealing his Virginian background—as easy to detect as if it had only been a few days since he left his native state. "Matter of money?"

The boy showed insulted anger. "I ain't no thief—no more than I'm a murderer. But Fairoaks folk figure I'm both. Reason I have to have your horse, mister. You get down off of him."

Steele saw the exhaustion in the boy's handsome face now, mixed in with fear. And, although he never shifted his unblinking glare from Steele, it was obvious he was listening for new sounds in the surrounding trees.

"The horse I can replace, son," the Virginian responded evenly. "But he's carrying a big investment. And the rifle's priceless in my book."

"Just get off him, Goddamnit!" the boy commanded, his voice rising to a shrill note.

Steele pursed his lips, nodded, and swung out

of the saddle. Despite holding the upper hand, the boy was terrified. Not of Steele, but the Virginian knew that was immaterial. The youngster who had the drop on him was in some kind of trap and would allow nothing, or nobody, to stand in his way of escape.

"That's better," the kid rasped when Steele was on the ground. The gelding continued to drink, relishing the coolness of the water. "Now you back over to the center of the clearin', mister. And don't you pull nothin' fancy. My life's on the line so I ain't got no pity to spare for a stranger."

Steele did as he was told and the boy moved away from the oak to sidestep around the pool, all the time maintaining his rock-steady aim on the target.

"Folks in Fairoaks say I killed a man, mister. A real important man—mayor and all that. They catch me, they'll string me up from the closest tree."

"Won't have to look far," Steele drawled, dark eyes raking around the timber-enclosed clearing.

The boy's arm wavered for part of a second, as he held the Colt one-handed to grip the horn and swing astride the saddle. The gelding had finished drinking and made no complaint as the new rider mounted. Steele had no time to crouch for the knife; just enough to reach into a pocket of his suit jacket and draw out a pair of gloves. Black buckskin, old and dirty and scuffed. That contoured every line of his hands as he pulled them on.

For a moment, he thought the initial action of taking out the gloves had spooked the boy. The youngster was in the saddle by then and his finger actually moved against the trigger. But then he expressed only a puzzled frown as he saw Steele start to pull on the gloves.

"Kind of good luck charm," the Virginian said evenly. "Always wear them when there's trouble."

The boy shook his head. "You ain't in no trouble, mister. Not if you keep doin' like you're told. Town of Fairoaks is about four miles northeast. If you miss it, there's a trail goes off on both sides so you won't get lost."

"You want me to be grateful for the information, son?" There was just a hint of irritation in Steele's voice now, as he faced the realization that he might indeed lose his horse and gear.

"Just want to tell you the truth to that lynch mob that's out to get me, mister!" came the angry response. "If I was a murderer like they say, I'd have just blasted you and took what I wanted. But I ain't no murderer. You tell them that!"

He gathered the reins one-handed, then froze as he was about to jerk on them to wheel the horse. The natural noises of the forest had suddenly ceased, as ears more sensitive than those of Steele and the boy picked up distant sounds of a new intrusion. For a moment, the two men in the clearing heard nothing to disturb the perfect stillness. Then, from far in the northeast, came the thud of slow-plodding hooves and crackle of breaking brush.

Fear reformed the boy's features into ugliness again. "You tell them, mister!" he rasped, his voice low. "And you tell them I was real sorry to steal your horse this way."

He wheeled the horse now, and dug his heels to

drive the animal toward the timber at the southern side of the clearing. As he did so, he had to turn in the saddle and aim the Colt across the front of his body.

The heat of Steele's anger at the prospect of loss was swamped by the ice cold fear of dying from a bullet. But it was a tightly controlled fear that put a sharp edge on his actions and negated the recklessness that anger would have triggered. He powered down into a crouch as the boy started to turn. The split in his pants seam gaped and his gloved hand streaked into the opening. It came clear in a blur of speed and when the gun drew a bead on him again, the knife was already spinning through the air. The throw had been underarm, the swing of the throwing hand given extra impetus as Steele sprang up from the crouch.

For a split second the boy's terror was totally detached from the lynch mob that could be heard coming through the trees. He saw Steele in the process of straightening, a grimace of effort stretching the skin of the Virginian's face drumtaut. He also saw something glinting with sunlight in midair between himself and Steele. And it was fear of the unknown which sparked the new assault of terror in his mind. For that brief slice of time, he knew he was being attacked, but did not understand the meaning of Steele's action or realize that it was a spinning knife blade that reflected the sunlight.

Steele threw himself to the right. The aimed Colt started to track him. The wooden-handled knife thudded its four inch blade into the flesh of the boy's left shoulder. He grunted with the shock

10

of the impact and squeezed the trigger by reflex action.

The bullet cracked across the clearing and thudded into a tree trunk. The gelding had started to lunge forward and the boy was hurled from the saddle, arms and legs flailing. His grunt became a shriek, that was abruptly curtailed as he hit the water of the pool and submerged.

Steele rolled once and powered erect again, venting a whistle that brought the gelding to an abrupt stop.

The boy came to the surface of the pool, the water splashed by his thrashing arms stained pale pink by his own blood. He was no longer holding the Colt.

"Mister, you gotta help me!" he yelled as he grabbed at tufts of grass on the pool bank, his plea cutting across the sounds of disturbed water and the abruptly fast progress of riders spurring their mounts into a gallop through the trees.

Steele was ambling toward the gelding. "What did you ever do for me, son?" he asked softly as he picked up the reins, his voice too low to be heard above the more frantic sounds.

"They'll lynch me for sure!"

The Virginian led his horse over to the pool, dropped to his haunches and eyed the wounded, terrified youngster with a total lack of compassion. "So there doesn't seem much point in hanging on to life," he muttered, put a gloved hand around the knife handle, and jerked the blade clear of flesh.

The boy screamed in agony and hurled himself backward, blood spurting to billow like dark smoke in the pool above his writhing form. Steele

11

wiped the blade on the grass, returned the knife to its sheath, and stood up. The boy broke surface, choking on water, and kicked forward to re-establish his hand-holds.

"Leave him be!" a man bellowed as he led a group of horsemen out of the timber, all of them reining in their sweat-lathered mounts and springing to the ground.

Steele turned casually, his dark eyes calm and expressionless now that the anger and fear had drained out of him. He saw ten men, of assorted ages from mid-twenties to early sixties. All of them grim-faced but just one with a revolver drawn to threaten the Virginian. He was the man who had roared the order, the only one to wear a gunbelt around his waist. The others carried an assortment of handguns jutting from pants belts and waistbands. None wore a badge.

From their garb, Steele picked out two storekeepers, a blacksmith, a barber, a telegraph operator and, maybe, a bartender. The other four were dressed in sturdy work clothes that did not advertise their business. It was the blacksmith who drew a bead on Steele as he advanced across the clearing. A man in his upper forties with a face that seemed to be covered with the same brand of leather his apron was made of, with pale blue eyes and a squashed nose, his jaw darkly bristled.

"Our business is finished, feller," the Virginian told the advancing man as the others moved into a tight-knit group behind the blacksmith.

"What was your beef with Ford?"

Steele shook his head and showed a sardonic

grin. "No beef. Matter of a horse. Mine. He tried to steal it."

"Please, Mr. Wallace!" the boy implored. "I didn't kill Mr. Fuller! I swear to God I didn't murder him!"

Wallace turned his Remington .44 and his cold stare toward the boy in the water. "When did God ever mean anything to you, you little bastard!" he snarled. Then his eyes narrowed as he saw the stained water and bloody shoulder. "Hey, get him outta there! He's hurt."

The barber and one of the storekeepers ran forward. Ford swung his desperate gaze from Wallace to Steele and his eyes were mirrors of his tormented mind as it raced to decide between drowning himself or surrendering to another brand of inevitable death.

"It's your fault!" he screamed at Steele, and tried to thrust himself out from the bank.

But he had used too much time in trying to stir the Virginian into remorse. The young, blond-headed storekeeper grasped his wrist and yanked the doomed Ford back into the bank. The boy shrieked in agony as his wounded shoulder took the full force of the wrench. Then he began to sob as the elderly, baldheaded barber grasped his other arm and he was dragged up onto the bank.

"Got him, Noah!" the barber announced breathlessly.

Ford began to writhe and kick, interspersing his sobs with shrill curses and deep-throated pleas for his life.

"He fire at you?" Wallace asked, eyeing Steele and ignoring the struggle as more men moved to restrain the fighting, yelling Ford.

13

The man who wore the green eyeshade that marked him out as a telegraph operator had gone in the opposite direction, to where the group of horses were cropping on the lush grass of the clearing. Steele watched idly as the tall, thin, hollow-cheeked man lifted a coiled lariat from a saddle.

"In self-defense, I reckon," the Virginian answered. Ford had become silent now, following the crack of a powerful fist against bone. "He was on my horse and riding. My knife was almost in him by then."

Wallace spat into the shaded pool, where the water was already becoming clean and clear again. "Sorry you was bothered by him. And you can consider yourself lucky, stranger. Hour ago he shot down a man in cold blood, stole from him and took it on the run."

Steele nodded and swung up into his saddle. "Told me you'd say that. Asked me to tell you he stole my horse without harming me. That was the way it was supposed to be, but the situation changed."

The lariat had already been fashioned into a lynch rope. With calm deliberation, the telegraph operator tossed the noosed end up and over a thick branch of the oak. "Get a horse, Boyd," he said evenly.

Ford had been stunned by the blow and remained on the brink of unconsciousness for long enough to have his wrists tied behind him with his own belt. Most of the men backed away from him and the bartender went off to fetch a horse. As he was forced to his feet by the storekeeper and barber, the boy stopped being hysterical and

14

now seemed petrified as he watched the calm preparations for his death. Tears, sweat and water from the pool merged and coursed down his lean, handsome face.

"Emmet Ford killed Martin Fuller sure as sunrise every mornin', stranger," Noah Wallace growled, nodding his satisfaction with what was happening, then returning his steady gaze to Steele as he holstered the Remington. He shrugged his broad shoulders. "Fact that he didn't try to kill you until you started somethin' just shows what a tricky bastard he is. Never been anythin' else. Figured we'd have second thoughts about him killin' Marty if he let another man live, I guess."

"No," Ford rasped softly, unable to prevent himself being dragged toward the horse, which was held below the branch with the rope looped over it.

"Advise you to be on your way and not interfere," Wallace continued when Steele did not reply.

"Your problems aren't mine, feller," the Virginian answered, moving to take up the reins.

The telegraph operator lowered the noose and Emmet Ford groaned and sagged between his captors as the bartender adjusted the circle of rope around his neck and tightened the running knot to a snug fit.

"But you should know something, stranger!" the man said quickly. He was one of those who did not reveal his line of work by his dress. The oldest of the lynch mob, he must have been close to sixty, with a ring of white hair atop his hatless head. Short and paunchy, with gnarled hands and

15

skin like crinkled brown paper. His voice was strong and urgent. "We are normally law-abiding people! If there was any doubt in a single mind, this terrible thing would not be done!"

Wallace nodded emphatically as the whole group except himself and the old man moved to aid in raising the sobbing, struggling boy onto the horse. "Mr. Menken's right," he told Steele. "This don't seem to bother you none, but I guess you ought to know. Wasn't nobody else but Ford could have killed Marty Fuller."

The condemned man was astride the saddle now and had become rigid again, as the rope was drawn taut, from his neck up to the branch, over it and then down into the willing hands of the telegraph operator. To struggle might result in premature death—before some kind of miracle could save him. His lips moved in a silent prayer for the miracle, the only sign of animation in an otherwise frozen face.

"And maybe if it wasn't Mr. Fuller that was murdered," Menken went on, "we would have waited for the sheriff to get back and handed Ford over to the law."

"Let's get on with it, Noah!" the eyeshaded man holding the rope growled. "It ain't no concern of the dude. And he don't look like he gives a damn one way or the other."

The fresh, sweet smells of the timber permeating the hot air in the clearing were suddenly masked by the stench of human excrement.

"Shit scared, are you, Emmet?" the young storekeeper taunted, grimacing as he backed away from the terrified boy.

"Abby Grover'd sure know you were a stinker

if she was here now!" another young man added, and laughed.

He, the young storekeeper, the barber and two others went to join the telegraph operator in holding the rope.

Menken ignored the sour and gleeful remarks as he continued to peer intently at Steele through the thick lenses of his spectacles. "Fairoaks is a nice town filled with nice folks," he insisted. "And today it lost one of the finest men that ever drew breath—all for the sake of a few dollars stolen by this ungrateful wretch." Contempt began to drip from his words. "A boy who should have gone down on bended knees every night and morning to thank the man he slaughtered in cold blood!"

He shifted his gaze from Steele to Ford as he poured out the scorn. And his words penetrated the private world of misery which the boy had drawn about himself. Ford opened his eyes, curtailed his silent prayer and wrinkled his nostrils—only now becoming aware that terror had caused the filth to torrent from his bowels. He wrenched his head from side to side, the tautness of the lynch rope restricting the movement. But he was able to see the men beside the horse and, beyond them, Steele, Noah Wallace and the elderly Menken.

"I didn't!" he croaked. "I swear by all that's holy I didn't take a cent. Please, don't! . . ."

Sobs rose to trap the words in his throat. Then he retched, and vomited.

"Do it!" Wallace snarled.

Somebody cracked a hand on the flank of the horse and the torrent of partially digested food

17

hitting its neck acted as a further spur to the animal. It lunged forward with a snort of complaint. The men holding the rope tightened their grip and tensed their muscles to take the strain.

"No!" Emmet Ford screamed, then was silent except for the sharp crack of his breaking neck as his body fell free and was pulled up short.

His body shook in spasms and was then limp. His head hung at an unnatural angle as the whole dead weight swayed gently.

A couple of men smiled but the rest remained grim-faced. One groaned, but whether from relief or remorse, it was impossible to judge.

"Lower him," Wallace ordered, and the men handling the rope complied, allowing the corpse to sink slowly to the grass—as if feeling a degree of respect for the corpse of a boy they had only hated while he was alive.

"Doc Pollock?"

The middle-aged man who crouched beside the crumpled form and felt for a pulse did not look like a doctor. "He's dead, Noah," he reported. "It's done."

He hooked his fingers under the noose and loosened the rope to remove it from the head.

"Sorry you had to see that," Wallace muttered to Steele. "This ain't the kinda impression of Fairoaks people we want strangers to get. On account of it ain't a true one."

"You told him to leave, Noah," the telegraph operator growled as he recoiled the killing lariat.

"But things got kinda hectic before he had the chance, Herman," the blacksmith rasped.

With the exception of Herman, the younger storekeeper and the freckle-faced man who had

18

taunted Ford with a woman's name, the lynch mob were suffering pangs of regret about their participation in the brutal killing. And Wallace, who seemed to have been the leading force, appeared to be engulfed by more self-reproach than any other.

Steele remained unmoved by the exchange, then showed just mild surprise as the elderly Menken approached the corpse, taking a clerical collar from his pants pocket as he knelt down. As he fastened the stiff, slightly grubby collar about his neck, he sensed the Virginian's watching eyes and turned his head to meet the quizzical gaze.

"He swore upon everything that is holy. But to this wretched boy nothing was holy while he was alive. Nevertheless, every departed soul deserves a prayer."

He clasped his hands together and bowed his head to deliver such a prayer, his words just a mumble against the resumed sounds of the forest's wildlife. Most of the other men from Fairoaks removed their hats and inclined their heads. The preacher's ankle bone cracked as he finished and rose to his feet.

Steele had held the gelding quiet and still while Menken pleaded forgiveness for the sins of Emmet Ford. Then he tugged gently on the reins to turn his horse away from the pool.

"If you're lookin' for a good place to rest up the night, stranger," Wallace offered, "Fairoaks is a fine, clean town."

"But a sad one," Menken added as he removed the starched collar and replaced it in his pocket. His face seemed to grow longer with melancholy, as if he were giving a demonstration of the

19

town's feelings. "Following the sudden and tragic demise of Mr. Fuller."

Some of the others nodded in solemn agreement.

"Grateful to you, feller," the Virginian answered as he urged the gelding slowly forward. "But that's not the kind of mourning I like to wake up to."

CHAPTER TWO

Steele kept to the northwestern course he had been traveling when he reached the clearing. He rode as easily as before. The afternoon was peaceful once again, the foliage of the giant redwoods and trees of lesser stature keeping the brush-covered floor of the forest pleasantly cool. The face of the Virginian was displaying its familiar impassiveness.

Nothing had changed, except that a young man named Emmet Ford had died. But the lone rider had witnessed death many times previously, on a greater scale and amid more horror than today. And a large number of these deaths had resulted more directly from his own actions than that of the young boy who had just been lynched.

There had been much dying in the War Between the States, but the horrors of that long-past conflict were almost forgotten memories now, having no influence on the Adam Steele who rode through the timber country of northern California. Except—he was prepared to admit on the few occasions when he considered who, what and why he was—that the Civil War and his experiences in it had enabled him to survive the violent peace which followed.

And a survivor was what he was.

The component parts of who he was had, of course, started to form long before the war. The son of a rich Virginia plantation owner who had acquired the taste for the good things of life, with the money and manner to enjoy them. Then a fine soldier in the Confederate cavalry, when his horsemanship, skill at shooting and natural leadership qualities had been used to good effect as a lieutenant. During the bitter struggle, made harsher by the fact that his father's sympathies were with the Union, he had learned to kill without pity and, sometimes, without honor.

Had fate allowed it, he was prepared to forget the lessons of war when peace finally came; to heal family wounds and take up the kind of life which had been his before the attack on Fort Sumter. But destiny had mapped another course for him.

His father, wrongly accused of a heinous crime, was brutally murdered on the same night that Abraham Lincoln was assassinated. And Adam Steele fired his first shot of the violent peace, the recoil of which sent him half way across the continent, searching out the killers of his father and forcing them to pay for their crime—using the war-taught lessons he had intended to forget.

At the end of that blood-drenched killing trail he was wanted for murder, and had been forced to kill his best friend to avoid arrest and trial.

There had been remorse then, which he had sought to drown with hard liquor in the cantina of a tiny Mexican village. But the alcohol had merely numbed the anguish and it had taken a

22

long time on another harsh and blood-run trail before he could even think about forgiving himself for killing Deputy Sheriff Jim Bishop.

And that trail, criss-crossing the vast, near-emptiness of the far and south-west was the "why" of Adam Steele's harsh existence. Because it led nowhere, his goal destined to be ever out of reach; for his acknowledged impossible aim was to re-establish for himself the kind of life he had experienced before the war and that which he had sought to live afterwards.

But he could never return to the Steele plantation, which he had last seen as a burnt-out ruin, because the old murder charge barred his way. All he could do was to drift from one place to another in the west, trying to make enough money to indulge his penchant for the good things, with a damaged dream that the impossible would one day come to pass. Constantly aware that fate was punishing him more severely than the law if he had returned with Bish.

For his ruling destiny decreed that trouble and danger should accompany him almost everywhere he chose, or was driven, to go. And, on the few occasions when he had come near to establishing a semblance of what he once had been, the opportunity had been cruelly snatched away from him.

As he had ridden down from the Sierras toward his meeting with the doomed Emmet Ford he had felt more contented than he could remember being in a long time. There had been bad trouble and a lot of danger in the silver mining country of the Snake Mountains in Nevada. But Steele had handled it, once again making use of his war-taught skills honed toward perfection by his peacetime struggle to survive. And, when it was over, he was richer by several thousand dollars.

And he still had the greater part of the money, after investing in a new horse and saddle, a replacement for a lost knife and a complete outfit of the dudish clothes he favored. In his mind there was a notion to get to San Francisco; either to use his large stake for a period of fine living at a plush hotel, or to finance some scheme which could make him even richer.

It was no more than a notion because past experience had taught him never to make firm plans until he was around the next turn in a trail or had crossed from one side of a town street to another. And the episode in the clearing had been an example of the potential dangers which were constantly thrust in his path toward the impossible.

As he continued to ride easily through the redwood forest, looking for a place to make the coffee which had been denied him at the clearing, he acknowledged that a change *had* come over him since the lynching of the boy. He was no longer whistling; and this because his contentment with the present state of his life had slipped a few degrees as a result of what had happened.

Not because of the fact that Emmet Ford had died. Instead, because of the way the boy had died, and the accident of his name. On the night Lincoln was shot, Benjamin P. Steele was summarily lynched in a bar room across the street from Ford's Theatre in Washington.

Steele did not need such coincidental events to trigger memories of the grief and suffering in the distant past, and he could now recall the death of his father and its traumatic aftermath without anguish torturing his mind. Thus, his change of mood was caused merely by the parallel in the manner of the death of a man and a boy. And the Virginian, who was normally unmoved by violence, found himself unable to ignore the possibility that the similarity went beyond the actual lynching; that perhaps the boy had been as innocent of the crime as the man had been.

It was late in the afternoon and the shade of the forest was a good deal cooler when he reached the bank of a narrow, shallow stream. He lit a small fire and unsaddled the gelding, then made and drank a pot of strong coffee. The sun sank lower and as the shade deepened, the fresh smelling air with its pleasant aroma of coffee cooled still more. Steele's mind continued to be nagged by a dissatisfied conscience which refused to accept the excuse that Emmet Ford had been a total stranger to him. By a combination of accident and design, he had contributed to the circumstances which enabled the lynching to take place. And Emmet Ford could well have been as guiltless as Benjamin P. Steele.

So the Virginian did not remove his gloves after he had doused the fire, resaddled the gelding and mounted. For, although he did not intend to seek out trouble, he was aware of the possibility that it might arise. And, as he had told the boy, he regarded the gloves as a lucky charm—the sole piece of imagery in a life that was otherwise totally devoted to stark reality.

He had first started to wear them during the war and was not now able to recall the precise circumstances which had led him to think of them in the way he did. The knife sheath in his boot and a split in his pants leg—which had a far more practical application—also originated from the war. The Colt Hartford rifle, which he prized in second place to his life, was the only inheritance he had received from his father. And it still bore a gold plate on the rosewood stock, with an inscription proclaiming its origin: TO BENJAMIN P. STEELE, WITH GRATITUDE—ABRAHAM LINCOLN. The kerchief with weighted corners had been captured from one of several vicious Oriental killers who had tried to stop him getting his revenge against his father's murderers.

These few items, plus the shabby sheepskin coat which he donned before continuing his ride, were the only tangible possessions he had carried out of the distant past. The other necessities of life and survival against his enemies and the elements, he obtained and discarded as he moved along the endless trail to nowhere.

When he emerged onto a road which cut from east to west through the dense forest, the sun was close to touching the far-off peaks of the Coast Range of mountains. But it had not yet started to change its color from yellow to red and, without the filtering effect of foliage, its heat still had traces of earlier harshness.

As was his way, Steele had no concrete plan in his mildly troubled mind as he turned his back to the sun and heeled the gelding into a restrained canter, heading toward the town of Fairoaks. But he felt he had to find proof of the guilt of Emmet Ford before he put the area behind him—or for a long time to come his mind would not be free of doubt. And, on the dangerous course destiny had mapped out for him, it was vitally important that he should be able to devote his entire, unimpaired concentration to looking for an dealing with each threat to his survival.

Fairoaks was still, he estimated, some two or three miles to the east when he reached the small farmstead. The first indication he had that he was nearing the place was the smell of wood-smoke in the air. Then he reached the end of a long curve in the trail and saw the cluster of buildings set amid neatly kept fields, the whole situated in a five-acre plot claimed from the forest, on the south side of the road.

There was a single story house—little more than a shack—a barn and a stable, all of log construction. The buildings stood some twenty feet back from the road, with a picket fence along the entire front of the property. On the other three sides, the cornfields were bounded by red-woods. Behind the barn there was a small piece of wire-fenced grazing land, shared by two milk cows and a pair of gray mares. Immediately in front of the buildings was a yard, half of which was hard-packed dirt and half devoted to a flower garden. A flatbed wagon was parked in front of the barn. Double gates in the picket fence were wide open.

Close to the farmstead, Steele smelt the appe-tizing aroma of cooking ham rising from the house chimney with the woodsmoke.

"Good evenin' to you, stranger," a woman called brightly as the Virginian drew level with the gateway.

He reined the gelding to a halt and it was an automatic gesture that raised his hand to touch his hat brim. The house had two windows at the front, one either side of the porched entrance door. Both gleamed from polishing and were hung with lace curtains. The door was open, but he did not see the woman until she stepped from the dim interior of the house onto the porch. She was in her late fifties, as neat and clean and homely as her surroundings. Tall and thin, she had a kindly face that had never been beautiful. Now it was burnished and lined by weather and the passing years. She had gray hair, held in a tight bun, but this did not make her look severe. Her dress was white and red gingham, largely hidden by a crisp apron of gray denim.

"Certainly is a fine one, ma'am," Steele replied.

"But been a hot day. The kind after which a cold glass of fresh-made lemonade goes down well, I guess?"

Her smile was bright and took several years off her true age as it lit her green eyes and parted her lips to display very white, even teeth. Steele responded with a smile of his own as he dismounted and he too looked younger for the expression: almost boyish and totally at odds with the killing instincts that were latent behind the outer shell of the man.

"You've invited yourself a guest, ma'am," he told her as he led the gelding across the yard and hitched the reins to the wagon in front of the barn.

He took his hat off as he neared the woman, and saw that his first impression had been correct but lacking in the finer details. She was the age he had guessed, she was thin and she was plain; and she smelled as fresh and clean as she looked.

But there was something about her smile—mostly generated from her eyes—that he did not spot until he was close. There was a vacant quality to her face, like that of a young baby who still had much to learn of life.

"Well, you come right ahead inside, son," she invited. "Guess a young feller like you are won't get no romantic ideas about me, seein' as how we're all alone here until my boy gets back."

She vented a girlish laugh as she swung around and swayed into the house. Her voice sounded different when it was not raised to shout, and her laughter seemed out of character with a woman of her years. Following her over the threshold, Steele added all these factors together, combined them with what she had said, and reached the conclusion that his hostess might be a little simple-minded.

"Here you are, son. Help yourself. Be obliged if you'd pour me a glass."

She had seated herself in a rocking chair to one side of the range on which the ham was cooking. The room was small, a combined kitchen and parlor, with doors leading off at each side. The furnishing was meager but well-made and cleanly kept, centered around a table with a straight-backed chair at each side. On the table, spread with a gingham cloth the same pattern as the woman's dress, was a jug of lemonade and two clean glasses.

"Grateful to you," Steele said, and took off his gloves before he poured from the jug into both glasses.

"If you want to sit, use one of them there chairs," the woman instructed, taking the glass

29

he offered her and waving her free hand toward the table. She nodded to a second rocker on the other side of the range. "That there is my boy's place. Only right the man of the house should have a chair special to him, ain't that so, son?"

"Sure," Steele acknowledged, and sipped the cool drink. He remained standing.

Outside, the evening had already put quite a chill in the air. The house was overheated by the fire in the range.

"My boy'll be home pretty soon now. But you don't have to fear him none. He's a good boy and he'll believe me when I tell him you been the perfect gentleman with me."

"That's good," Steele told her, and started to drink the lemonade faster, regretting the impulse that had led him to accept the woman's invitation. He looked everywhere but at the woman, sensing her amused eyes gazing at him.

"Usually gets home before this time from his place of work in Fairoaks. But a man called here and told me he'd be late. Hope you're enjoyin' the lemonade, son. Guess I'm showin' Fairoaks folks ain't the only ones can be hospitable in this neck of the woods. Ain't that so, son?"

"Sure," the Virginian said again. "I'm grateful to you."

"The man that called before you. He wouldn't have no lemonade. Was in kind of a hurry to get off. But I was mighty glad to see him. Brought me this, to show my boy'll be home soon."

There was a deep pocket in the front of her apron. She delved into it and brought out a worn leather billfold. Steele had finished the lemonade and had turned toward the woman to thank her again. He saw that her smile had gone and been replaced with a look of mixed sadness and something akin to shame.

"Might be a message in it, but I don't read too well, son. Fact is, I don't read at all. I got confused by what the man said. Be mighty obliged if you'd see if there's a message and read it to me." She held out the billfold toward Steele, a plea in her eyes. "Should be addressed to me. The message, I mean. Name's Mrs. Rose Ford."

Steele showed no response to the name as he took the ancient billfold out of the woman's scrubbed, slightly trembling hands. And his face stayed impassive as he opened it and looked at the sparse contents: a one dollar bill and a torn and faded photograph of the woman taken not too long ago.

"No message, I guess?" Mrs. Ford muttered. "Emmet wouldn't write to me, would he, son? Him knowin' I ain't never had no learnin' to let me read." She turned her sad gaze toward the still open door, then the smile brightened her features again. "But he'll be back soon. Why don't you pour yourself another glass of lemonade?"

"No more, ma'am," Steele replied, closing the billfold and handing it back to her. "Real grateful for the first. Goodbye, Mrs. Ford."

She made no move to follow him immediately. But as he mounted the gelding after unhitching the reins from the wagon, she appeared in the doorway of the house again.

"If you see my Emmet, you tell him to hurry, you hear? Supper's cookin' and I don't want it to spoil." She laughed. "But best you don't tell him

31

you came in the house. He might not like it his ma entertained a gentleman while he was away."

Steele touched the brim of his hat, walked his horse across the yard and did not demand a canter until he was out on the trail, heading east again.

The lemonade, which had tasted so refreshing inside the neat little house, felt bitter in his stomach. The surrounding forest, cool and pleasant during the day, seemed more cold than it should have been at evening, and permeated with latent menace. But the Virginian knew the bitterness was created by his own sense of guilt and that his mind was conjuring up imaginary evils in the towering trees; that he was experiencing the dangerous response of doubt he was going to Fairoaks to eradicate. Or confirm.

He rode by other small farmsteads, with windows lamplit against the gathering gloom. None as well tended as the Ford place, and he neither saw nor heard anybody.

If Emmet Ford had killed the town's leading citizen, Steele knew he would be able to forget the dead boy and the simple-minded mother left to take care of herself. If he had not . . . The Virginian had survived the heavy burden of guilt which came from cold-bloodedly murdering his best friend. So the knowledge would be easier to handle than the doubt.

He put on his gloves as he came in sight of Fairoaks, after passing a half dozen small farms spaced out along both sides of the trail. A single street town of entirely timber-built properties, all of them single story. Where the trail became the unnamed street, it broadened to twice its width and was flanked by neat, clean, solidly constructed buildings for about five hundred yards, before narrowing into the trail again. At a midway point along the street, a stream cut across and was spanned by a timber bridge.

The buildings close to the water-course were business premises—a hotel and saloon, four stores, a livery and blacksmith, stage line and telegraph office and barber's shop. All these had sidewalks in front of them. Elsewhere there were houses, enclosed by fencing and standing amid flower and vegetable gardens. At the eastern end of town there was a church with a stunted steeple on one side of the street and a meeting hall on the other side. There was a cemetery beside the church.

When the redwoods and brush were cleared to make room for the town, the California oaks had been left untouched. They dotted gardens and rear lots and two of them arched the stream with their branches where the water ran between a dry goods store and the hotel on the south side of the street. Across from this, a side trail spurred away between the blacksmith and livery and a butcher's shop, to disappear into the trees, following the same course as the stream.

There was no sun now, and lights gleamed brightly from many windows, haloed by the vapor of a gentle mist. It was very quiet and the cool, slightly moist air was redolent with wood-smoke and cooking smells. Hastily made wreaths or pieces of jet black fabric hung on every door.

Steele held the gelding to a walk along the center of the street, sensing that the steady clop of slow-moving hooves drew curious gazes toward him. But nobody appeared until he halted his mount in front of the Wallace livery and blacksmith's shop. Then the batwing doors of the Fairoaks House were pushed open and Noah Wallace hurried out and across the street. He had washed up and shaved and changed from his working clothes into pressed pants and a freshly laundered check shirt. His pale blue eyes were lit by a friendly smile as he reached to take the gelding's reins from Steele as the Virginian dismounted.

"Glad you changed your mind, stranger," the blacksmith greeted. "I'll take care of him, for you. You head on over to the Fairoaks House. Order what you like and you won't have to pay for a thing."

Steele relinquished the reins, but drew the Colt Hartford from the boot. The act erupted a troubled look across the leather-textured face of Wallace.

"You won't need that in this town, Mr.—?"

"Steele. Where I go, it goes. Come to be a habit."

Wallace shrugged his massive shoulders. "Just as you like, Mr. Steele. And I guess you can do exactly what you like in this town without folks complainin'."

"I'm not owed a thing," the Virginian growled. "But I'd be grateful for some answers."

The blacksmith nodded vigorously. "Sure. Be a pleasure. I'll bed down your horse and be right over to join you."

The livery doors were not locked and as Wallace opened them and led the horse inside, Steele

34

started across the street. His expressionless eyes moved over the signs above various business premises. Fuller's Grocery to one side of the hotel. Across the bridge was Sherman's Dry Goods and, beyond this, Harry Farnham's Hardware. Opposite the grocery store was Frizzell's Fine Meats. Then, across the spur trail, came Wallace's dual business, the stream, Reed's Barber Shop and the stage line and telegraph office. The pole-strung wire connected to this building stretched out along the trail in both directions.

When he pushed through the batwings to enter the small saloon section of the Fairoaks House, he saw he had been correct in guessing the line of work of the thirty-five-year-old man named Boyd. Red-haired and dark-eyed, the medium-built man was behind the short run of bar to one side of the saloon.

Boyd was grinning, arms stretched out in front of him and hands grasping a shot glass and whiskey bottle on the counter top. "This your pleasure, mister?" he called brightly. "It's the best in the house."

"The house sell coffee?" Steele asked, not responding to the buoyancy of the bartender.

A shake of the head with the grin still in place. "Not to you, mister. You get it give to you—for nothin'."

Steele advanced to the bar and rested the rifle on its polished wood top, dug a dollar bill from his inside pocket and placed it beside the gun. "I'll pay my way."

Anger abruptly replaced the grin on Boyd's face. "It ain't polite to insult generosity, mister," he rasped. "Folks around here are just naturally kindhearted and they——"

"I've seen what folks around here are like," Steele cut in. "I'll pay my way. A man can get killed by kindness."

CHAPTER THREE

"Don't beg the guy, Marv. He wants to pay, let him pay."

Steele had already seen and recognized the quartet of patrons seated at a table near the saloon's large front window. The man who gave the advice was the telegraph operator named Herman, looking just as he did in the afternoon, except that he no longer wore the green eyeshade. The scowl on his thin, hollow-cheeked face seemed to be a permanent fixture. He was in his late twenties, balding prematurely.

He shared the table with the two storekeepers who had been at the lynching, and Reed, the totally bald barber. These three men had changed out of their working clothes. All of them were drinking beer and smoking cheroots. A half empty beer glass on the bar close to where Steele waited marked the position where Noah Wallace had previously stood.

"No offense intended, feller," Steele said softly as the bartender continued to glower at him. "But I'd be grateful if you'll sell me a cup of coffee."

Boyd snatched the bottle and glass off the bar top and returned them heavily to a shelf. "Suit yourself."

He moved angrily along the bar and pushed open a swing door to go from sight into the rear of the place. Steele used up time by glancing around the room which, in front of the bar counter, was furnished with just six tables each ringed by four chairs. Half a dozen lamps were bracketed to the walls and a pot-bellied stove stood at one end, just beginning to radiate heat. An arched entrance at one side of the bar was labeled Hotel and at the other end were double doors lettered RESTAURANT AND COFFEE SHOP. The walls, ceiling and floor were all wood.

"I'm Herman Thornberg," the tall, thin man announced to end a long period of silence. "This here's Oscar Reed, town barber. Harry Farnham who owns the hardware store. And John Sherman, likewise the dry goods business."

"Adam Steele," the Virginian supplied to keep another pause from growing long.

"I'm stage line agent in Fairoaks," Thornberg went on. "And look after the telegraph office as well."

"Don't reckon I'll need the services of any of you gentlemen," Steele said, and turned back to the bar as Boyd reappeared with a smoke-blackened coffeepot and a tin mug.

"You want a room?"

"Maybe."

"Put the cost of the coffee on your bill."

Steele replaced the dollar in his pocket, leaned his rifle against the nearest table and then sat down, to pour coffee into the mug. Boyd went out back again and the quartet of beer drinkers began to talk in low, secretive tones.

The blond-haired Harry Farnham was the

38

youngest of the four, a squint-eyed, pale-faced man in his early twenties. The freckled John Sherman was in the same late-twenties age group as Thornberg. Oscar Reed, slightly built with a round, red face, was about fifty-five.

While he sipped the coffee, sensing frequent surreptitious glances in his direction from the window table, Steele recalled the lynching in the forest. It had been Thornberg and Reed who did most of the manhandling of Emmet Ford. And Farnham and Sherman had delighted in taunting the condemned youngster.

Everyone else in the shady clearing shared the responsibility for what had happened. But the four men across the saloon were the only ones who had appeared to derive some form of sadistic pleasure out of the lynching.

"Just what exactly do you need in Fairoaks, Steele?" Thornberg asked at the end of the low-voiced discussion. "We seem to recall you were dead set against coming to town."

"He's got some questions need to be answered, Herman," Noah Wallace supplied as he pushed in through the batwing doors. He strode toward his half-finished drink, raised the glass, drained it at a swallow, and banged it down on the bar top. "Marv!" he yelled. "Refill!"

The bartender hurried out from the back to meet the order, as Wallace dragged a chair away from the table opposite Steele, and lowered himself wearily into it.

"Real fine horse, Mr. Steele. And he's getting the treatment he deserves. Left your gear over there at the livery—on account I'd like to ask you to stay at my place. No sense in haulin' it over—"

"Room here if I need one," the Virginian interrupted as Boyd leaned across to thrust a foaming glass of beer into Wallace's outstretched hand.

"Just as you like," the blacksmith allowed.

"Made it plain he does what he likes, Noah," the bartender growled. "And figures to pay for it."

Wallace grimaced, first at Boyd, then turned his head to show the same expression to the now silent and expectant quartet of men near the window. "I said this feller could have anything he wanted, within reason. That means he can do whatever the hell he likes . . ." He returned his level, open gaze to the neutral set of Steele's features. "Within reason."

"Like I've already said, feller, I'm not owed a thing here."

Wallace nodded. "I guess we'd have caught up with the kid even if you didn't happen along. But you made it easier for us. Don't matter, though. You want to turn down local folks' hospitality, then that's all right."

"Had some hospitality out at the Ford farm," Steele said, freshening his coffee.

Harry Farnham vented a cackle of laughter. "Some lemonade, I bet! And lots of talk about you not taking her into the bedroom and scre—"

"Leave it be, Harry!" Wallace snapped, then softened his expression and tone. "It's a damn shame about Rose Ford. But maybe she won't ever know, her being the way she is."

"She thinks her son is coming home," Steele said. "Somebody took his billfold out to the farm."

"That was me," Wallace answered. "I tried to

40

tell her, but it wasn't no use. Like always, she just kept tryin' to get me to drink her lemonade and actin' like a flirty little girl. Never has been any different. She's seen folks in this town a thousand times, but never recognizes any one of them."

"Even used to try that vampin' stuff on with her own boy, I heard him tell," Marv Boyd supplied. "Sometimes never even recognized Emmet."

"Rose Ford'll be all right, Mr. Steele," Wallace assured. "That brute of a son of hers lived there and ate there but he never did a lick of work. Crazy old Rose does it all, and does it well. Like you saw. Ain't a better—"

"You find the money?" the Virginian interrupted.

"Money?"

"That Ford was supposed to have stolen from the man he's supposed to have murdered."

"Now, see here, Steele!" Thornberg snarled, whirling away from the bar where he had carried the four beer glasses to get refills. "That sneaky bastard done everythin' we said he did. Ain't no *supposed* about it!"

Wallace sighed and sipped his drink. "You want to take over, Herman?" he asked evenly.

"I just don't like this dude's high-hat attitude, Noah!" Thornberg countered. "He's actin' like some big city lawyer."

"Right, Noah!" Oscar Reed agreed. "With us the guilty parties."

Boyd nodded while Sherman and Farnham voiced their agreement.

The blacksmith made placating gestures with

splayed hands, still looking at Steele, his back to his fellow citizens. "A man can't help the way he is. And ain't no sense anybody flyin' off the handle on account of a little thing like a man's manner." He listened for a moment to the silence this introduced into the saloon. Then he nodded his satisfaction, and sighed as he drew a pipe from his shirt pocket and began to tamp tobacco into the bowl.

"How would it be, Mr. Steele, if I told you exactly the way of things? How they been up to today, and how they happened today? That oughta answer all your questions without you havin' to even ask them."

"You the new mayor?" Steele asked evenly.

Wallace showed a slight smile but, just beneath the surface of his easygoing attitude it was possible to see the effort he had to make to retain his self-control. "The old one. But that don't mean I got a God-given right to run things here in Fairoaks. No more than Marty Fuller when he was alive, or Sheriff Jesse Cutler when he's in town. We got us a town council." He shrugged. "But things happened kinda fast after Marty got killed. The local folks just naturally looked to me—on account the sheriff was out of town and I used to be mayor, I guess. And there weren't no time to call a meetin' before we took off after Ford."

"And it's worked out fine so far," Marvin Boyd growled. "Everybody's happy the way Noah handled things."

Thornberg had returned to the table and set down the refilled glasses. "Except some of us

42

think he don't have to make no apologies to you, Steele!" the hollowed-cheeked man snapped.

"It ain't costin' any of us any damn thing!" Wallace countered, then returned his gaze to Steele. He quickened his voice, as if anxious to get his talking over before there was time for further interruptions. "You already heard what folks think—damn, thought—of Marty Fuller. Only fair you should know Emmet Ford was far away the most unpopular feller hereabouts. Been that way almost from the day he brought his mother out here into the woods. Two years ago, about?"

He glanced around at his fellow citizens and they nodded in confirmation.

"Had a bankroll which was enough to buy the small place out on the west trail. Didn't stretch to supplies, though. And when some robberies happened, it was plain the boy was guilty. Specially since he straight away started buying stuff for the farm."

"Acted as simple-minded as his ma," Harry Farnham muttered scornfully.

"Hadn't have been for Marty Fuller, Ford would have been run outta town or maybe even arrested and tried for the crimes. But Marty took to the boy for some reason—God knows what it could've been. Made good the money that was stole, and give the boy a part time job in his grocery store. Paid him more than he was worth, it seems. After him and his ma got the farm going —and everyone allows they made a fine job of that—it made enough money to keep them. But not enough to pay for so many round trips to San Francisco and medical bills."

Wallace paused to drink some beer, then hurried on again before Steele could pose a question.

"Rose Ford wasn't always simple in the head. She got that way after an accident of some kind in the city. Appears she could die if she didn't have this special kinda medical treatment every six weeks or so."

"Never would have been able to have it," Boyd put in, "hadn't have been for Marty Fuller taking on her son and paying him double what he was worth."

Wallace nodded and relit his pipe. "And Emmet never did show any appreciation for what Marty did for him and his ma. Got drunk whenever he could steal a bottle and made a nuisance of himself—firin' off his gun inside town limits, startin' fights with other youngsters and insultin' women. Gambled with any passin'-through strangers that were a mind. Disappeared for days on end with never a word about where he'd been."

"Real wild little bastard!" Thornberg growled.

"And Marty knew it as well as everyone else," Wallace went on. "But if Marty had one fault, it was stubbornness. After he took the boy under his wing, wasn't nothin' could happen or nothin' anybody could say to make him change his mind."

"Plenty happened and plenty of people said things," the town barber muttered sadly.

"That's about how things were up until today, Mr. Steele. Then, this afternoon, we heard a shot from the back room of the grocery store. We all rushed over there and found Marty dead with a bullet in his head. Safe was open and cleaned out. Papers all over the floor and every last cent missin'. Menken was last one to reach the store. He'd been up on the church, fixing the roof, and he saw Ford take off into the timber right after the shot was fired."

Wallace seemed to have finished, as he raked the burnt tobacco out of his pipe bowl. But he looked up suddenly.

"You asked a question, Mr. Steele. And I have to say that we didn't find no money on Ford, apart from just the one dollar in his billfold. But he could have hid it in a hundred places between town and the place we found him. Folks are goin' out to take a look tomorrow."

Steele had drained the coffeepot dry as he listened to the story, the air within the small saloon growing thick with tobacco smoke from Wallace's pipe and the cheroots of the other customers.

"The whole of what Noah just told you is the truth, mister," Boyd said.

"So you can see there was no doubt Ford killed the mayor," Reed added.

"Still don't see why it's so important a stranger has to know about Fairoaks business," Thornberg snapped.

"Grateful to you," Steele said as he stood up, and transferred the coffeepot and mug to the bar top. "Just one other question."

"Happy to oblige," Wallace assured, then showed surprise when he saw the Virginian was looking toward John Sherman.

"Who's Abby Grover?" Steele asked the freckle-faced owner of the dry goods store—the man who had taunted the doomed Ford with the name of the woman.

"The girl who preferred Emmet to him!"

45

A draught of cold damp air across the stove-warmed saloon accompanied the opening of the batwing doors. The voice of the newcomer, which drew every pair of eyes toward her, seemed to chill the atmosphere far more.

She was in her early twenties, a petite redhead, no taller than five feet with a figure that managed to be slim but generously curved; apparent, despite the short-length, thick coat that was tightly buttoned from her throat to midway down her thighs. She also wore Levis of the same drab gray color, riding boots and a Stetson hat. Her hair fell in long, natural waves at either side of her face, to reach below her shoulders. The features it flanked were well-formed, dominated by a pair of large, bright blue eyes. Her lips were full and her jawline had an aggressive thrust, at odds with the quality of softness that was possessed by the rest of her facial structure. She was pretty, with the promise of beauty that would come with maturity.

As she moved into the well-lit room, it could be seen that her eyes were red-rimmed from recent tears. Her expression was as hard and icy as her voice.

"Doc Pollock told me what you all did to Emmet!" she snapped, halting in the center of the small room and turning slowly, to rake her harsh gaze across every face.

"The Doc had to go out to the Magoffin place, Noah," Boyd supplied.

"I know that, Marv," Wallace answered. "And I told him to stop by at the Grover farm."

Like the other men who had been seated when Abby Grover entered, he did not rise in the presence of the woman. And all the local citizens met her harsh eyes with equanimity. The Virginian expressed curiosity. First, as she glanced at him as part of the small crowd, then as she returned her attention to him.

"You're the one stopped Emmet getting away?"

Steele was standing between the bar and the table he had shared with Noah Wallace. As she spoke, the woman advanced on him, her expression and tone of voice becoming more bitter.

"Tried to steal my horse, ma'am," Steele answered levelly.

She had thrust her hands deep into her coat pockets since entering the saloon. Anger made her as rigid as a stone carving when she halted, just a foot in front of the Virginian. Her clothes and hair smelled of damp timber from her ride through the forest and it was a fresh, pleasant aroma in the smoke-heavy atmosphere of the room.

"Go home and do your mournin', Miss Grover!" Wallace advised, his tone making it almost an order. "And spare some tears for Martin Fuller."

The woman ignored him as she continued to stare hatefully into Steele's bristled face. "I can't do anything about the people in this lousy town, mister! There are just too many of them. And they stick together like wolves in a hunting pack. But you're a stranger here. And maybe more to blame than they are. So I—"

Her big eyes were a gauge to her anger. Steele saw the fierce emotion building in them, then dropped his quizzical gaze. In time to see her right hand move inside the coat pocket. On the periphery of his vision, he saw Wallace close to the four men at the table in the background. Every face showed an expression of detached curiosity laced with a degree of expectancy.

Steele raised his left hand, as if to rasp gloved fingers across his day's growth of beard. Instead, he shot the hand forward, splayed out to cover the woman's face. And lunged to his right as he made contact and pushed. Behind him, he heard a gasp and the thud of Marvin Boyd's footfalls as the bartender scuttled away from the trouble.

A small caliber gun cracked, the bullet exploding a black-ringed hole in the woman's coat. She was going backward then, driven by the force of Steele's one-handed shove. The backs of her thighs collided with the edge of the table where Wallace still sat and she was tilting when she squeezed the trigger, so that the bullet left the small gun on an upward trajectory, lifting a splinter of wood from the top of the bar before it ricocheted to smash a polished glass on a shelf at the back.

She screamed in alarm and rage as she sprawled backward across the table, struggling to free her hands from the traps of the coat pockets.

Wallace continued to sit stoically on the chair as the woman's writhing body tipped the table away from him and shed her to the floor. Her scream became a shriek that sounded like the start of an obscenity, but then was abruptly curtailed as the back of her head crashed against a chair seat. The heels of her boots hit the floor first and the rest of her was limp in unconsciousness when she was spread-eagled on the boarding.

Steele sensed, but did not see, a degree of disappointment about the watchers as he went forward to squat beside the inert woman.

"Real little hellcat, ain't she?" John Sherman growled.

Steele eased Abby's hand from the right side pocket of the coat, then he delved inside and drew out a single-shot, .22 caliber derringer, its barrel still warm from firing. There was nothing fresh-smelling about the woman now, the acrid scorching of the coat material masking all else.

The Virginian put the gun back into her pocket and picked up his Colt Hartford, which had been knocked to the floor as the table tilted. He blew dust off the barrel and wiped the stock with a gloved hand. "She and Ford were a good match, uh?" he asked Wallace.

The blacksmith had managed to snatch up his beer glass before the table was disturbed. Now he drained it of everything but foam before he answered.

"Fairoaks has an ordinance against whores, Mr. Steele," he replied quietly. "But folks always reckoned that if we didn't have that, Abby Grover'd be first to set up in business. But I don't believe that personally. She had a lousy start here in this town. Last big trouble we had before today was when Abby was raped by a drifter came through here. She wasn't but thirteen then. Harvey and Leroy—her two brothers—took off after the man that done it. Never did say whether or not they caught up with him."

He handed his glass to Boyd for another refill and started to push more tobacco into his cold pipe. "Anyway, after Abby got to looking like a

49

woman instead of just a little girl, lot of men around here figured she was fair game. And she played their game—just up to a point, I figure." He shot a scornful glance over his shoulder toward Sherman. "Some men that get turned down by a woman feel their pride's been hurt. And them kind sometimes put it around they didn't get turned down. Shoot off their mouths they got what they wanted and called it a day."

"The hell with that, Noah!" Sherman growled in angry defense. "You ever hear that hellcat deny what was said about her?"

Wallace lit his pipe and blew out a stream of smoke. "Never did," he said, looking at Steele. "But then Abby thinks a lot of them brothers of hers. And knows they think a lot of her."

He raised his eyebrows in a tacit enquiry. Steele had taken the dollar bill from his pocket again and now he placed it on the bartop.

"They wouldn't take it easy, uh?"

"Sure wouldn't, Mr. Steele. And when one citizen of Fairoaks is in trouble, the rest rally round."

Boyd had taken the dollar and piled change in its place. Steele picked up the coins, but his nod was directed at Wallace.

"She wasn't too angry to forget that."

"Folks on the out-of-town places are regarded as citizens, Mr. Steele. If she had shot you, we'd have rallied around her, I guess. You ain't stayin'? Here at the hotel, or my place?"

The rifle made his chore awkward to accomplish, but Steele managed to get both arms under the limp form of Abby Grover and raise her from the floor.

50

"Any reason I should?" he asked.

"Been a long, hot day," Wallace answered. "And a man needs to rest. We'll take care of her and see she gets home safe."

The Virginian shook his head as he raked his impassive eyes over the saloon's customers. All of them—even Wallace now—appeared completely indifferent to the stranger in town. "Like to handle my own troubles myself."

Harry Farnham laughed harshly. "You sure got your hands on a whole bundle there, dude. And Abby Grover ain't the kind that forgets easy."

Steele carried his unconscious burden toward the batwing doors.

"She don't talk a lot of sense about Emmet Ford, Mr. Steele," Wallace called after him. "Like Marty Fuller in that respect. Couldn't see no wrong in him."

"It'll make a change, feller," the Virginian replied. "After listening to people who couldn't see no right in him."

"I said he was a fine farmer!" Wallace snapped, then added. "When he was a mind to be."

"A warning, mister." Thornberg said, his voice almost a snarl, as Steele was about to push out through the batwings. "You better not come back here and try to stir up trouble if that little bitch sells you a bill of goods!"

Steele halted and looked back over his shoulder. The expression on every face allied the men with the skinny telegraph operator. Noah Wallace confirmed the solidarity with soft-spoken words.

"You turned down the hospitality of a fine town, Steele. We did our best to repay a debt we figured we owed you. Only natural folks ain't goin' outta their way to help you no more."

"Damn right, mister!" Oscar Reed put in. "We're even."

"I've got no argument with that," Steele replied, and pushed out through the doors into the mist-hung, chill night. Then lowered his voice. "But something sure is odd."

The woman in his arms uttered a low groan, but showed no further sign of regaining consciousness. He grinned down into her face, which was far prettier in repose than when she had been consumed by grief-inspired rage. "Struck you too, uh?" he asked wryly.

CHAPTER FOUR

Abby Grover's horse was hitched to a public water trough midway between the wooden bridge and the eastern limits of Fairoaks. Which explained how she had been able to reach the doorway of the saloon before anyone inside was aware of her approach.

But many other people in the quiet town, now shrouded in full night, had probably watched the woman's progress. As they watched Steele now, crossing from the saloon to the livery, themselves unseen but strongly sensed by a man who had often survived because he was able to detect such things.

In the livery, he laid the woman on a pile of hay while he saddled his gelding. Then, before draping her over the saddle and leading the horse outside, he placed two dollars under a coffee-stained mug on the battered desk.

It was easier for Steele to ride Abby's pinto mare than to transfer her to her own horse. And, as he rode, with the lead reins hitched to the horn of the pinto's saddle, he kept both horses side by side, one hand holding the woman in place.

If further proof was needed that she had ridden in along the east trail, the pinto had left hoof-prints in the mist-dampened dust of the street. They showed up clearly in the light spilling from windows, augmented by the softer moonglow. And this same combination of light illuminated both riders and their mounts until they were beyond Fairoaks, on the narrower trail cutting through the high timber.

In the trees there was just enough filtered moonlight to prevent the night being pitch black; but visibility was foreshortened by the thin mist, which dampened exposed skin and soaked clothing as effectively as a rain shower.

Lighted windows showed farmhouses to either side of the trail, looking much the same and spaced out at similar intervals to those west of Fairoaks. But the pinto mare showed no interest in any of them.

Steele had traveled almost a mile from the edge of town—and had ridden by three farmsteads—when he felt a stab of anxiety about his riding companion. He had seen and heard her fall hard, but she was young and healthy. So it was not until she had been unconscious for better than fifteen minutes, in cold and damp that should have had a rousing effect, that he considered the possibility she was seriously hurt, in the knowledge that he was taking her away from probably the only doctor for miles around.

The shot missed his head by a fraction of an inch.

He saw the orange stab of the muzzle flash out of the corner of his left eye. Against the gray and black background of the mist-entwined timber to the north of the trail. His feet were clear of the stirrups when he heard the crack of the rifle shot, and felt the slipstream of the bullet across his forehead.

Both horses pricked their ears, then snorted their displeasure at Steele's action. For he threw himself sideways, unbooting the Colt Hartford with one hand as the other fisted around the collar of Abby's coat to wrench the woman clear of the saddle.

The animals were spooked into a lunge of speed by the hectic, unsignaled activity, the falling forms between them forcing them apart.

Steele hit the ground hard, trying to cushion the woman's fall with his own body. Then, as soon as they were both down, he pushed her roughly away and rose into a crouch, cocking the rifle and aiming it into the timber.

Ears straining to hear sounds other than the beat of hooves, eyes peering without a flicker into gray-tinged blackness.

The muzzle flash of the second shot dazzled him for a split-second. But, as he heard the bullet smack into a tree ten feet to his right, he powered upright and squeezed the Colt Hartford's trigger. Careful not to move his head to left or right, he emptied all six chambers of the cylinder, aiming at the spot in the darkness where the retinas of his eyes continued to paint an orange splash in the night.

Through the barrage of shots, he heard Abby Grover groan, and a brief cry of pain that sounded more animal than human.

Ignoring the woman, he went forward, delving into a side pocket of his jacket for shells. He ran fast across the open trail, then trees and brush forced him to slow down. He spun the cylinder as he flattened himself against a trunk of a massive redwood. Hot shells fell to his boots and bounced onto the ground. As he began to feed fresh shells into the chambers, the woman groaned again and scratched at the ground. From further away, in the opposite direction, came another sound of pain. Definitely from a horse. Then a human voice called, urging the animal into speed.

His rifle fully loaded again, Steele swung around the massive trunk and struck deeper into the timber. For thirty feet, he was struggling through snagging brush. Then he stepped out onto a pathway, not wide enough to allow two horses to pass—formed by a constant trampling of the brush. Something gleamed in a stray shaft of moonlight angling down through the trees. And, as he stooped to pick up an ejected rifle cartridge, his glove became smeared with a sticky substance.

The shell was .44 caliber, probably ejected by a Winchester. A struck match showed the staining on his glove to be blood. There was more of it on the ground; one large splash and then several smaller patches to point the direction in which the rifleman had gone—westward. More blood than a man could lose and still have the strength to ride. It tallied with the cry of pain he had heard and meant that a bullet from the Colt Hartford must have hit horseflesh.

The forest was silent except for the groaning of Abby Grover, the rifleman long gone astride his wounded horse. Steele tossed the shellcase away, losing it in the brush where another one was hidden, and back-tracked to the trail. The woman's groans had a more histrionic ring the closer he came to her and, when he stepped out onto the trail, he saw why. While pretending to be in the grip of paralyzing pain, Abby was fumbling to push another shell into the derringer.

When she looked up and saw him emerge from the timber, she vented a shriek of alarm and tried to snap the gun to aim at him. But she forgot the locking lever and the barrel folded downward.

Steele grinned at her as he canted the Colt Hartford to his shoulder. "Just not your day, ma'am," he said as he advanced on her.

She was sitting in the center of the trail, where she had landed after being jerked off the horse. Her legs were splayed and she was aiming the tiny gun two-handed, arms at full stretch in front of her. The Stetson had fallen off her head and was hanging down her back. She looked feminine and vulnerable minus the hat, and did not struggle when Steele leaned down and plucked the derringer from her hands.

"You?" she said hoarsely, confusion clouding her pale face. "What's happening? Why am I . . . where did you come from?"

There was still some hatred behind the confusion, and it became more firmly re-established with each passing moment.

"Usually ask a lady if I can take her home," Steele answered, glancing along the trail to where the mare and gelding were quietly cropping at grass—all panic gone. "But you were in no condition to say yes or no. Somebody else had an objection, though."

She massaged the back of her head, and winced as her fingers put a sharper edge on the pain. "I remember. You hit me!"

Steele ejected the shell from the derringer, snapped the gun closed and dropped both into the pocket of his sheepskin coat. "Not the way I like pretty women to fall for me," he told her.

He held out a hand to help her up, but she said something under her breath and struggled erect on her own. For a moment or two, she swayed and seemed on the point of collapsing. But she controlled it.

"What do you want?"

Steele sighed. "First things first, Miss Grover. Somebody just took a couple of shots at me. Or maybe he reckoned to kill us both. Either way, the first thing I want is to stop being a sitting duck for him to try again."

Abby was recovered sufficiently—and was enough of a woman—to fluff up her hair before she replaced the hat on her head and dusted off her coat and pants. But her hostility remained at a high pitch.

"I think it more likely somebody else was bringing me home—and it was you who ambushed us."

Her big eyes raked the immediate surroundings, searching for evidence to back up the contention.

"Why would I do that?" he asked, and turned his back on her to stroll toward the docile horses.

"I tried to kill you!" she snapped after him.

"I'm too old to follow the examples of other people, ma'am."

The reins of the gelding had become unhitched from around the horn of the pinto mare's saddle. Steele slid the Colt Hartford into the boot and swung astride his own horse.

"You coming?" he asked, looking back along the trail to where the woman was standing stock-still, hands on her hips in an attitude of defiance.

"You can go to hell, mister! I've already been there, when I heard what happened to Emmet!"

The Virginian leaned forward and gathered the reins of the mare. "I'll wait for you at your place. But you'll have to walk. Need your horse to show me where you live."

"Horse thieves get hung around here! But in your case, Leroy and Harvey might blast you full of holes first—when they see you've got my horse!"

"The Grovers sure sound like one big impulsive family, ma'am."

He started the gelding forward at an easy walk, tugging on the reins of the mare to urge the second animal to follow. Behind him, the woman remained unmoving for long seconds. Then she spurted into a short, fast run. Just far enough to narrow the gap between herself and the Virginian to about twenty feet. Then she matched the pace of the horses. Steele glanced over his shoulder at her twice, and both times her pretty face was set in an expression of burning hatred. On the second occasion she emphasized her feeling toward him with an unladylike spit into the grass at the side of the trail.

"Was riding along minding my own business," Steele said at length, not looking back at her. "Ford pulled a gun on me and tried to steal my horse. Had to put a knife into him to stop that happening. Lynch mob moved in then and strung

59

him up. He wasn't hanged for being a horse thief."

Her response was another, more vocal spit, which Steele heard but did not see.

"They told me why they did it and I didn't have any good reason not to believe they were telling the truth. Reckon they all thought they were. But I had a crazy reason for wanting to check it out. That's why I was in Fairoaks—and why I'm here now. Talking to myself."

Abby confirmed that he was doing just this; for she did not even respond with a spit this time. But, when he glanced back over his shoulder, he saw that she was maintaining the twenty-foot gap as she continued to trail him.

He became as silent as she then and there was just the regular thud of shod hooves against damp-softened dirt to disturb the peace of the mist-shrouded timber country. Until, some fifteen minutes later, the mare gave a low snort of expectation as the horse smelt familiar scents. Less than a minute after this, Steele saw a light gleam among the trees on the left. The trail made a sharp turn in that direction, and ran across a clearing, the trees having been felled on both sides to give space for fields. The farm buildings—a large single-story house, two barns and a stable—were on the right. There was only one fenced-off area, forming a corral out at the back of the stable and barns, separated from the rear of the house by a yard on which two flatbed wagons were parked. The front wall of the house was only the width of the stoop away from the edge of the trail.

"I reckon this is home?" Steele asked as the mare exhibited more signs of recognition.

Abby said nothing and did not meet his gaze as he turned once more to look at her. There was suffering inscribed upon her pretty features now and her breathing was a little ragged; the self-imposed walk taking its toll upon her after the long period of unconsciousness. Her lips moved and made no sound, as if she was telling herself not to give in to the strain. And her eyes had a glassy look.

"Pa always said a good horse was of greater value to a man than any kind of woman," the Virginian growled at the mare.

"Surprised you got to know your father that well, mister!" the woman said, provoked to break her long silence. Her voice sounded reedy with weakness, then she gaped her mouth wide; perhaps to suck in a great gulp of the damp air, or perhaps to shriek for the help of her brothers.

Whatever, the strain finally told on her. The blue eyes snapped closed, the slender body became limp, and she crumpled hard to the ground. Steele pursed his lips, sighed, reined the gelding to a halt, and slid from the saddle.

"Hey, inside!" he yelled toward the house, which was still some hundred feet away. "You're needed out here!"

There was a muffled shout in response, which was not directed at Steele. Then the door, to the left of the lighted window, was flung wide. Two big men leaped out of the house, their bare feet slapping on the stoop, then hitting the trail. Each of them carried a rifle, both muzzles pointing in

Steele's direction, wavering as the men lumbered toward him.

"Hey, that's Abigail's horse!"

"Damn right, Leroy! And ain't that . . . hold it right there, mister!"

Harvey skidded to a halt, slamming the stock of the Winchester into his shoulder to draw a rock-steady bead on Steele. His brother kept right on running, veering to the side to give the Virginian a wide berth.

"It's Abigail sure enough!" Leroy reported anxiously as he squatted beside the limp, crumpled form of his sister.

"Harvey was fifteen feet from Steele, aiming a rifle capable of killing a man over a far wider range, if the marksman was skilled—and this one looked as if he knew what he was doing.

"Harvey, he looks like the dude Doc Pollock spoke of!" Leroy growled, as he came erect with his sister cradled in his arms.

"Mister, you sure have got some talkin' to do," Harvey muttered with heavy menace.

Steele nodded. "Be happy to . . . if folks will listen."

"You'll get a hearin', mister. After we heard what Abigail has to say."

"Looks to me like she's just plain beat, Harvey," Leroy announced as he carried his sister over the final stretch of trail to the open front door of the house.

"Be grateful if you listen to me before she wakes up, feller," Steele said to the brother with the aimed Winchester.

"You just bring them horses and hitch them at the side of the house, mister. You do that slow and easy. And keep your lip buttoned until I tell you Leroy and me are ready to hear you. Out here in the timber, we grown used to peace and quiet."

Steele knew there was not a chance that he could reach his rifle or knife before a bullet smashed into him. So he moved cautiously to the front of the horses and picked up both reins. "If your sister wakes up in the same mind she passed out, you'll get better than peace and quiet from me, feller," he muttered.

"How's that?" the puzzled Harvey Grover asked.

The Virginian showed a sardonic grin. "Dead silence."

CHAPTER FIVE

Inside the large, well-furnished parlor of the house, Steele could see that Harvey was about five years older than his brother. He was in his mid-thirties and was as handsome as Abby was pretty. A little under six feet tall, he was broadly built and his shirt—open at the neck and with the sleeves rolled up—contoured more muscular flesh than it revealed. He had a well-weathered, ruggedly carved face with eyes of Grover family blue. But his hair was jet black.

His brother was a slightly scaled-down model of himself, with a weaker mouthline and eyes that failed to indicate the same degree of high intelligence. Leroy's hair was matched in color to that of Abby, but heavily greased.

Both men looked the farmers they were, but they had not stopped working when they came in from the fields. They had washed up, but not shaved; and if they had eaten supper they had made a neat job of clearing away after the meal. Now, the big table in the center of the parlor was littered with books, papers, two pens and an inkstand.

Steele guessed it was Harvey who was teaching Leroy to read and write.

"Sit down there, mister!" Harvey ordered.

Leroy was not in the room, which was brightly lit by three kerosene lamps—two on the mantel above the hearth and one on a bracket on the facing wall. But, as the Virginian was urged into the house under the threat of the pointing Winchester, another lamp was lit to show a softer light at an open doorway.

Steele moved to sit in a high-backed Windsor armchair to one side of the blazing log fire as Harvey closed the front door of the house.

"She's got one hell of a bump on the back of her head, Harvey," Leroy called through the doorway of the softly lit room.

"Fix her up," his brother replied, and turned a chair away from the table, to face Steele, then sat down.

Leroy came back into the parlor, shot a hostile glare toward Steele, then opened yet another door. The smell of a recently cooked meal wafted through.

Harvey rested the Winchester across his bulky thighs, but with the muzzle still aimed at the Virginian and his finger hooked around the trigger.

Steele's mist-dampened clothes began to steam from the fire's heat as he glanced around the room with idle curiosity. It was much larger than the room at the Ford place, and served just the one function. The central table had four chairs around it. There was a Windsor comb-backed armchair to either side of the fire. A lowboy was backed to one wall, a bookcase another and a chest on yet another. One door—which presumably led to a bedroom shared by the brothers—remained closed as Leroy hurried out of the kitchen with a basin of steaming water and some cloth.

The furniture of the room was homemade, but skillfully done. It was intrinsically plain, but Abby's influence could be seen in elaborately patterned covers, frilled window curtains, painstakingly made rugs and a wide range of glass, pewter and porcelain ornaments.

A pillar-and-scroll clock on the mantel chimed the hour of nine to end a long silence which had been marred only by the splashing of water in the woman's bedroom.

"Just a lump on the head, far as I can tell, Harvey," Leroy said as he came out into the parlor and closed the door quietly behind him. "Best she sleeps a while, I figure."

The elder brother nodded. "Leroy's just startin' to learn readin' and writin'," he told Steele. "But he has a natural bent for dealin' with sick people."

Leroy showed something close to pride for a moment. Then the former hostility crowded back into his eyes as he lowered himself gently into the armchair opposite Steele. He was about two inches shorter than his brother, slightly narrower in build, but nonetheless probably weighed half as much again as the lean Virginian. His dullness of brain was reflected in his features, robbing them of the handsomeness that was possessed by Harvey.

"You give Abigail that lump, mister?" he demanded, his voice quiet but threatening.

"All right to talk?" Steele asked the elder Grover.

Harvey nodded, solemn rather than menacing.

"Serve as well as anythin' to kill the time until Abigail wakes up."

Not much time was used by the Virginian giving an account of the day's events since he rode into the clearing with the pool. Leroy became pensive as he listened. Harvey's mood changed only once, when he asked for the derringer to be given to Leroy. He was tense and watchful until he saw the tiny gun was unloaded. Then melancholy as he said:

"It belonged to our mother. Father gave it to her when they first came out to the West. I'd forgotten it was still around the house."

There wasn't much for Steele to tell after that: Just about the rifleman in the timber, and he exhibited the blood-stained glove as some kind of proof it had happened. And of their sister's intransigence that had inflicted the exhausting walk upon herself.

There was a long pause after the tale was told. Then Harvey nodded.

"Abigail always has been the mule-headed one in the family," he allowed. "Once her mind is made up, it's like trying to fell a redwood with a Bowie knife to get her to change it."

Ever since the derringer had changed hands for a second time that night, Harvey had failed to hold the Winchester in a threatening manner. Now, he lifted it from his thighs to place it on the littered table.

"Seems to me it was Abigail that was at fault, Harvey," Leroy said with a thoughtful frown. "If this here feller's tellin' the truth. He had the right to protect himself. And he didn't have to take the trouble to bring her home. Specially after he was shot at again."

"That's right, Leroy," Harvey agreed softly, his blue eyes appraising the Virginian carefully.

Steele submitted calmly to the survey, aware that the man studying him had the ability to mine beneath the surface impression and read the character that lay beneath.

"And he ain't told us why he did that. Nor why he sidetracked himself to Fairoaks instead of headin' the way he was goin'."

The Virginian had been reasonably relaxed since it had become obvious the Grover brothers did not intend to kill him out of hand. Then, as their hostility diminished and the warmth of the fire made the damp and cold night outside just a bad memory, a sense of well-being had eased all the tensions of the afternoon and evening out of him. In such a situation as this, Steele was inclined to look far younger than his true age. His face became almost boyish, losing many of the signs of harsh experiences and all indications of the latent killer instinct that lurked within him: telltale marks at once subtly and blatantly apparent when danger threatened.

Perhaps Harvey Grover had spotted the true character of the man out on the moonlit trail when he aimed a gun at Steele. Or maybe his ability to judge his fellow men was so finely honed that he could see through the thin outer shell without previous clues to what lay beneath.

"And he ain't the kind that would cross the street to help a dyin' man unless he had a good reason, Leroy." His voice was still low, but heavy with contempt. However, his light blue eyes held only a question.

Leroy was puzzled, but remained silent.

Steele could not be insulted by the truth so he accepted the scorn calmly, then gave his reasons for going to Fairoaks and in bringing Abby home; and there was more than one now. The second having more substance than the mere coincidence of a lynch mob and a name, involving as it did a motive for murder no stronger than Emmet Ford robbing a man who had always been his benefactor. And the third was the most solid of all—based on the foundation of the two bullets aimed at him from out of the timber.

As the Virginian began his explanation, the door of Abby's bedroom had been cracked open. There was no accompanying sound and Steele was the only one of the trio of men in a position to see the slight movement. And he did not refer to it until he said quietly:

"I hope there aren't any more guns lying around the house."

Both brothers were puzzled by the comment, until they turned in response to Steele's nod. Her eavesdropping discovered, the woman had swung the door wide by then, and stepped from the bedroom into the parlor. Her red hair was still damp from where Leroy had bathed her injury, but there was no dressing on the bruise. Her skin was pale and her whole face continued to be haggard from strain. Leroy had taken off her boots and coat. The tight fit of her levis and blue denim shirt contoured a body that lived up to Steele's expectations of generous curves.

"You all right, Abigail?" Harvey asked anxiously as the woman reached out a hand to grip the doorframe.

Steele took off his hat, as much for his own comfort in the warm room as in deference to the woman. Leroy hurried up from the chair and went to help his sister. But she glowered at him as if he had done something wrong, and made it to a chair at the table without assistance.

"Make some coffee," Harvey instructed his younger brother and Leroy went into the kitchen, apparently pleased to have a chore to do.

"No worse than when I fell off the wagon runaway," the woman told Harvey, then stoked more fire into her glower and directed it toward Steele. "I got to allow that what I overheard makes a lot of sense, mister."

The Virginian acknowledged this with a slight nod. "Folks in town reckon I wouldn't get a lot of that out of you, ma'am. Not if you were talking about Emmet Ford."

The glower became a sneer, but although she continued to stare at Steele, the woman was no longer reacting to him. "Only three people in the world gave a damn for Emmet! One's dead. Another's crazy. And I'm the third. Everybody else either hated him or treated him like he was something crawled out of a rotted tree stump. So it's bound to be that Wallace and the others figure anything good said about Emmet is nonsense."

"Abigail's right, mister," Harvey confirmed as his sister became tightlipped in angry contemplation of the past. "I don't like Ford. Leroy neither. But he was his own worst enemy. Never did one thing to get himself liked."

"Because he wasn't given no chance!" Abby

snapped. "He was a little wild when he came here, on account of the lousy time he had in the city. And people around here—except for Mr. Fuller and me—never gave him a chance to change his ways. Everyone was so high and mighty decent and honest and hard-working they—"

"There's nothin' wrong with that," Harvey countered as Leroy entered with a tray loaded with steaming, aromatic coffee mugs.

"There is if folks like that expect everyone else to be exactly the same—even if the others ain't had all their advantages." Anger had suffused her cheeks with color and she added bitterness to the other emotion as she swung her gaze from Harvey to Steele. "I suppose them goody-goods in Fairoaks told you about what happened to me a few years back, mister? Well, maybe that's the reason I took a shine to Emmet. The real goody-goods gave me a bad time because I got raped and they figured that made me no better than some kind of whore—"

"Abigail!" Harvey rebuked.

"Shut up, Harvey!" his sister snapped, without turning her blazing eyes away from Steele's impassive face. "And some of them that ain't so goody-good tried to find out if I'd gotten a taste for being raped!"

"Drink your coffee!" Harvey insisted, and there was enough harshness in his tone to get through to the woman.

She shrugged and her rage diminished as she accepted the mug thrust into her hands. "Anyway, it meant that Emmet and me had bad times in common, mister. And people that have things

71

in common sometimes take a shine to one another."

Steele nodded his thanks to Leroy as he was given a mug of coffee. Then, as the first gulp flooded into his stomach, it reawakened the pangs of hunger he had not felt since Mrs. Ford had invited him into her house for lemonade.

"Fuller's bad times were long gone," he said pointedly. "If he ever had any."

"Martin Fuller was just a decent human being," Abby countered, then used a tone of voice that made her comment just as pointed as Steele's had been. "Some people don't have to have any better reason than that for helping other people."

"That why you think Ford didn't kill him, ma'am?"

The query plunged her into an anguished silence. Out of the blue, Leroy asked:

"What's your name, mister?"

"Adam Steele."

Leroy nodded, as if the answer had explained a great mystery.

"Abigail was in town when it happened," Harvey said, as a prompt to his sister.

Abigail shuddered at the memory, and stared into her mug. When she spoke, it was the first time Steele had heard her voice minus the harshness of either anger or hatred. "It looked bad for Emmet, I got to admit that. I'd just come out of the grocery store and there was nobody left inside except Emmet and Mr. Fuller. A few minutes later there was a shot. Mr. Menken was up on the church roof and he yelled that Emmet was running away into the trees. I rode straight

72

home then, figuring that Emmet might come here. But nobody came until Doc Pollock."

"She said she was ridin' into Fairoaks to see Ford's body," Harvey told Steele. "Leroy and me had no idea she was——"

"I knew it was almost certain Emmet shot Mr. Fuller," the woman interrupted. "But that was no excuse for lynching him the way they did. If you hadn't been there, I guess I wouldn't have used ma's gun. The whole town of Fairoaks killed Emmet and a town can't be killed. But if it hadn't been for you, maybe the town wouldn't have had the chance to . . ."

A sob rose into her throat and burst into an escape between her trembling lips. Tears squeezed from the corners of her eyes and coursed over her cheeks, pale again now that anger was gone. She stood up suddenly, knocking the chair onto its back. Then fled to her bedroom. The door slammed closed, then the bed creaked as she flung herself onto it. Her sobs subsided until they could no longer be heard.

"You think I should go to her?" Leroy asked into the silence.

Steele's stomach gave a complaining rumble.

"I think you should fix Mr. Steele somethin' to eat," Harvey suggested.

Once again, the younger Grover brother seemed happy that he had something to do.

"Seems like you've had a wasted trip," Harvey said. "If Abigail's prepared to admit Ford had to be guilty . . ." He shrugged and shook his head, his expression solemn.

"Chance I took," Steele answered thoughtfully.

"And your sister's opinion doesn't count for much against a couple of chances somebody else took."

"How's that?" the puzzled Harvey Grover asked.

The Virginian's face was grim for a moment, then expressed an easy grin. "Two shots in the dark."

CHAPTER SIX

Steele and Abigail Grover set off from the farm toward Fairoaks as the clock in the parlor struck the hour of ten the next morning. Her brothers were already out in a field across the trail, hoeing weeds from between the standing corn. The Virginian had been awake at dawn with the Grover men, after sleeping on a pile of rugs in the parlor, and had eaten a large breakfast cooked by Leroy.

Harvey had refused cash payment in return for boarding Steele, but had asked that the visitor wait until Abby awoke—and accompany her to town if she wanted to go. With no reason to hurry, and aware it was a payment of sorts for the Grovers' hospitality, Steele had agreed.

It was a long wait, but a pleasant one, sitting on the stoop as the sun rose higher and grew warmer; burning off the damp mist and allowing the fragrant and fresh smells of the surrounding forest to spring to life. At first the brothers sat with him, Harvey answering questions about Fairoaks and its citizens, sometimes amplifying his replies to cover ground Steele was not in a position to ask about.

Then, after they had gone to work, he

continued to sit in the rocker, considering his new knowledge in relation to what he already knew. None of it did anything to detract from the evidence pointing to the guilt of Emmet Ford. Neither did it add anything to that evidence. And, inevitably, the quiet-voiced conversation offered no explanation for the attempted murder of Steele, Abby or both of them. His reason for returning to Fairoaks was more concerned with this aspect of yesterday's events than his former desire to ease a potentially troublesome conscience.

When the woman finally stirred from her bed, after waking naturally from the long and energy-restoring sleep, she seemed fully recovered from the physical injuries. But grief continued to dull her eyes and, despite what she had said the previous night, she was still filled with resentment toward Steele.

She did intend to go to town, to view the body of the dead boy and then to go out to the Ford place to see his mother. But she had strong objections to riding in company with a man she still regarded as largely responsible for Ford's harrowing death. Harvey convinced her to do so, though, transmitting to her his genuine fear that the rifleman might still be gunning for her.

So, garbed in the full mourning attire she had made after hearing of Ford's death, she rode the pinto mare alongside Steele's gelding on the trail toward Fairoaks. Tightlipped and dull-eyed, she did not utter a word the entire journey; nor even look at him.

The stark black of her ankle-length dress and bonnet had the effect of enhancing her youthful attractiveness and, had his mind been less occupied with other things, Steele might have regretted her lack of warmth toward him. As it was, he was content to remain as detached from Abigail Grover as she was from him.

Passing the small farmsteads between the Grover place and town, it was obvious the news of yesterday's events had been well circulated. For the men in the fields and the women attending to the household chores showed keen but surreptitious interest in the couple riding slowly along the sunlit trail. No greetings were called out and curious eyes watched but were quick to concentrate on other things when there was a danger of meeting the even, indifferent gaze of the Virginian.

In Fairoaks, the atmosphere of mixed embarrassment and censure was much the same as that shown by the farming families: until the woman veered her horse away from Steele's mount and swung from her saddle in front of the neat house next to the Meeting Hall. A shingle on the green-painted picket fence announced: IRVIN POLLOCK— MD AND MORTICIAN.

As Steele continued to hold his horse to an easy walk along the center of the street, he saw Abby walk around the side of the house toward an outbuilding at the rear. Then, when he faced front again, he sensed the change of atmosphere. The street had been virtually empty before and it had been his well-developed sense of being watched that had warned him he was not welcome in the neat, clean, quiet town. But as soon as Abby left his side, women appeared at the windows and doorways of their houses, cleaning cloths in their hands and smiles on their faces. Further down

77

the street, in the area where the timber bridge spanned the stream, the sidewalks in front of the business premises became peopled with other women carrying laden shopping baskets. Menken called a cheerful good morning from the porch of his church. And, as the Virginian rode his horse over the bridge, Oscar Reed, Harry Farnham and John Sherman raised welcoming hands from behind the plate glass windows of their business establishments.

But, when Steele failed to respond to the warmth of the citizens of Fairoaks, it became apparent how false their feelings were. For, hurriedly and with some relief, they withdrew into moods that were either morose or sullen or melancholy—all of these in keeping with the black mourning garb they all wore. And all went about their business in this manner, as the Virginian swung from his saddle in front of the saloon and hitched the gelding to the rail before sliding the Colt Hartford from the boot.

Before he stepped up onto the sidewalk, he watched Abby Grover ride along the street, over the bridge and then away from him, toward the start of the west trail. Her face was pale again, and wet with tears from paying her last respects to Emmet Ford. She looked neither to left nor right, seemingly unaware of the overt interest of Adam Steele and the far more secretive attention of the townspeople.

Then the Virginian went between the open batwings and into the clean-smelling, sun-bright saloon which was empty except for the dark-eyed Marvin Boyd behind the bar. Unaware of the many changes of mood which the townspeople had undergone during the past few minutes, the bartender displayed a broad grin as Steele approached him.

"Fine morning and it looks like it's going to be another fine day," he greeted brightly. His shirtsleeves were rolled down and buttoned and he wore a black mourning band below his right elbow.

"Sheriff Cutler around to enjoy it?" Steele asked as he leaned the rifle against the front of the bar.

He didn't respond to Boyd's grin and the bartender subdued it but remained in a pleasant humor as he raised a coffeepot from a shelf below the counter onto the bar top. "Pay if you want, or just join me for free."

He brought his own half-empty mug into view. Then had to go out back to get another mug when Steele nodded.

"Still over in Jamestown," he called through the doorway. "He should be back today, though." He reappeared and poured coffee for the Virginian. "I'm like you, Mr. Steele. Not a man for hard liquor. You got business with the sheriff?"

Steele had heard from Harvey Grover that Cutler had gone to Jamestown—thirty miles west of Fairoaks—to give evidence at a circuit court. Grover had also warned that Jesse Cutler disliked Emmet Ford and respected Martin Fuller to the same extent as most other citizens of the town.

"Somebody took a shot at me last night," the Virginian answered. "Just reckoned to make an official complaint before I checked it out myself. This town being the kind of town it is."

Boyd expressed surprise. "While you were with the Grover girl?"

"That's right. But the bullet came closest to hitting me. He's a lousy shot, but maybe not that bad."

The bartender showed concern now, as he frowned. "Jesse Cutler ain't the best lawman in the world, Mr. Steele, and he's inclined to be real lazy. Especially when a stranger brings a complaint against somebody local. You got any evidence?"

"Didn't reckon to get any help from him," Steele answered evenly. "Just wanted to get my complaint on record before I started treading on toes. There are a couple of bullet-wounded trees out along the east trail. And somebody's got a horse with a hole in it."

The coffee was long made and had been off the stove some time. It was strong but almost cold and Steele finished it in two swallows.

"Noah Wallace is the vet as well as everything else he does around here," Boyd supplied. "Maybe he'll help."

Steele grinned bleakly and glanced toward the open doorway and dazzling brightness of the sunlight on the street beyond. "And maybe we'll have snow before noon," he muttered wryly. Then he shrugged. "Anyway, Wallace isn't around. If he was, I reckon he'd have been cheerleading the phoney welcome-back reception I just got. Since he fixed it up for me?"

His raised eyebrows added the query and Boyd appeared sheepish for a moment. Then he spat behind the bar, and the sound of moisture hitting metal told of a direct hit into the spittoon. "Sure he did! We had a bad day for trouble yesterday. We still got the sadness of Marty Fuller being dead, but Noah figured it was better to try to heal old wounds." He sighed. "But since you were shot at, I can understand why you ain't amenable to that, Mr. Steele."

Harvey Grover had gone into detail about why Fuller had been such a highly respected figure in Fairoaks and the surrounding timber country. He was old when he came to the town, and rich from the shipping business he had run in San Francisco. Once his grocery store was established, he became a generous benefactor. He had financed the building of the church and Meeting Hall, extended interest-free loans to anybody in need, built a schoolhouse out along the spur trail to the north and shown kindness in a thousand and one less expansive ways. But his greatest gift to the community was when, seven years previously, he had propped up the ailing timber-felling and saw-mill company that operated a few miles north of Fairoaks.

Had the company failed, the town would have been abandoned. For most of the townsmen worked in the lumber business. Those who did not, earned their livings supplying the families of the company men. And, if these families had moved away the traders would not have been able to exist on business from the scattered farms. So, with Jamestown being the next closest community, the farmers and their families also owed a vast debt of gratitude to the now dead man who had saved Fairoaks from extinction and taken not a cent in profit.

"But Noah will help if he can," Boyd went on

emphatically. "Just like most other people hereabouts if they're able. Ain't many of us'll be happy knowing there's somebody with murder on his mind amongst us."

He left his own coffee unfinished and moved along the bar to a gap in the counter at the end.

"That stuff in here last night with the Grover girl—we let that happen because we knew you could handle it. After you left, we chewed the fat a while. And there ain't no doubt but that Abby Grover'd be in real trouble if she'd put a slug in you, Mr. Steele."

"That's heart-warming to know, feller," the Virginian drawled.

Boyd nodded solemnly as he came along the customers' side of the bar. "Ain't no denying but you got the right to feel sour. You want to come on over to Noah's place? Maybe he's gone out to treat a sick animal someplace else. Sometimes leaves a note where he'll be if that happens."

Steele shouldered the Colt Hartford and trailed the bartender out of the saloon and across the street. Open interest was expressed by the few people about, but no questions were asked. With the damp mist long gone, puffs of dust rose around the men's boots. Far off in the timber to the north, some kind of steam-driven machinery at the sawmill thudded and hissed. Distance and the intervening trees muffled the sounds. Chimneys released woodsmoke from cooking-fires as the time for midday meals approached.

The double doors of the livery stable were closed, but not locked. The shade after the street crossing was welcome, despite the malodorous atmosphere of the place. There were five horses in the stalls, which was one less than there had been the previous night after Steele had collected his gelding. The two dollars he had left under the mug on the scratched desk were still there.

Boyd went to the desk and shrugged when he failed to find the expected note. "Guess Noah didn't figure he'd be gone long."

Steele ignored him and moved from one stalled horse to another, checking for wounds and traces of blood. None of them had been hurt.

"Just Wallace's horse gone?" he asked the frowning bartender.

"Noah owns five mounts. He trades in horses. The chestnut in the end stall is Mr. Menken's. In here because it went lame and Noah's trying to mend the leg. Noah rides whichever horse he fancies. I don't think you ought to be poking about in here with him gone, Mr. Steele. We just came over to see if he left a note is all."

"One more question and you can go," the Virginian said evenly, as he started to check the five unoccupied stalls. "Did you see anybody leave town after me last night?"

Boyd's nervousness was increasing by the moment, and he shot constant anxious glances toward the half-open doorway. "No. No, I didn't. Nor heard anybody. Closed up my place no more than ten minutes after you left. This is an early-to-bed town and it was as quiet as always all night. What you looking for?"

"Man who tried to kill me. If Wallace didn't treat a shot horse here—or isn't out taking care of one now—he'll have no reason to object."

The bartender swallowed hard and swung around to start for the doorway. "I don't want no part of it—not while Noah ain't around to say it's all right for you to do it."

"Grateful for the help you've already given, feller," the Virginian told him, and grinned as he watched the bartender head for the doorway. "Reckon there's no sense in two of us getting in trouble—for flogging what could be a dead horse."

His grin froze as he saw trouble inscribed into Marvin Boyd's face—staring out of the bartender's enlarged eyes and screaming in silence from the man's gaping mouth. But, before Steele was able to tilt back his head and look up into the hayloft which had captured Boyd's horrified attention, his mind blotted out the reality of the stable. And, mercifully, responded for just a split-second to the searing agony that exploded at every nerve ending in his body.

Then he was dragged down under the surface of a black sea of unconsciousness.

CHAPTER SEVEN

There had been pain in the brutal war fought for a cause; and much more during the violent peace when survival was the sole reason for existing. On battlefields in the east; in Mexico; in Texas; in the territories of Arizona, New Mexico and Utah; in the state of Nevada; on battle-scarred, once-green fields; in burning deserts; high on bitterly cold mountains.

All of it as much an experience to be learned from as everything else which had happened to Adam Steele.

When he awoke now, the most recent assault against him concentrated its pain at the point of impact and under his skull. It was bad, like a powerful hand was inside his head, rapidly clenching and unclenching, its effect harder to bear when the imaginary fist was uncurled.

He snapped his eyes open and blinked away sweat and tears. He remembered the circumstances an instant before he was hit and, as his vision cleared, he saw that little had changed. He was still in the stable with its pungent odors of horse-wet and droppings and rotted hay. The place shaded, except where a wedge of strong sunlight pierced through the half-open door.

Marvin Boyd was still with him, but the bartender was no longer nervous; no longer anything except dead. He lay like the cross-stroke of a letter T at the point where the finger of sunlight ended. On his back, legs together and arms at his side. Flies were feeding on the still-moist blood which had torrented from his slashed-open throat.

Although the Virginian's flesh was soaked with sweat as he fought against giving vocal outlet to his pain, his entrails felt ice-cold with mixed anger and fear. His hat was on the straw-littered floor at his side. As he struggled into a sitting posture and lifted it to put it on his punished head, he saw it had covered his knife. The whole length of the blade was crusted with drying blood. It was a reflex action—with no conscious intention to destroy evidence against himself—that caused him to sink the blade into the dirt floor and remove the blood before he thrust the knife back into his boot sheath.

From outside came the familiar sounds of the steam-driven machinery at the distant sawmill. There were no other noises.

The Colt Hartford lay on the littered floor a couple of feet away, alongside a pitchfork with the shaft newly snapped in two. He reclaimed the rifle and used it as a prop to get unsteadily to his feet. Then glanced up into the hayloft where Boyd had seen the attacker poised to deliver the blow. There was no way up to the loft from inside the stable but Steele had seen the outside stairway canting up an end wall that faced the spur trail into the timber.

"Hey, anybody know where Marv's got to?" a familiar voice yelled from across the street. "I'm in sore need of a beer!"

It was Noah Wallace and the big man sounded in good humor, despite the absence of a bartender to supply what was needed to slake his thirst.

"You ain't the only one, Noah!" Herman Thornberg countered. "Ain't he where he should be?"

"Saw him take that Mr. Steele into your stable a while back!" Oscar Reed called. "You still in there, Marv?"

"Thought I recognised Steele's horse," the blacksmith with many sidelines said, his tone quieter and somewhat pensive. "You check the livery, Oscar. I'll see if they're in the hotel."

The Virginian took one step toward the doorway, but had to halt as the stable seemed to tilt and the apparent slope of the floor threatened to throw him back down again. The footfalls of the town barber thudded against the wooden bridge and men's voices were raised. The pain inside Steele's head acted to scramble much of what was said. But the men seemed to be yelling for the dead bartender to attend to his business—in a mixture of good humor and mild irritation.

Steele gritted his teeth and tried to will his mind to regain equilibrium for his limbs and body. But, amid a fresh wave of agony, it allowed him no more than the ability to pull back the hammer on the Colt Hartford. For, when he tried to swing the rifle to aim it at the doorway, his whole body turned from the waist, and he had to stagger to the side to keep from toppling.

Then the door was pushed wide, and the corpse of Marvin Boyd was splashed with bright sunlight, except where the shadow of the bald barber fell across the head.

"Oh, dear God!" Reed gasped, and crossed himself. Then vented a high-pitched squeal of horror when he raised his bulging eyes and saw Steele half turned toward him.

"Don't believe what you see, feller," Steele tried to shout, but the words came out in a croaky whisper.

And the elderly man was not listening, anyway. He had whirled and was waddling across the broad street, as fast as his short legs would carry him. Shouting something that was unintelligible to the disoriented Virginian. But the group of men on the stoop in front of the saloon either understood him, or were able to see the cause of the excitement themselves through the open doorway of the livery.

Steele shook his head, and his vision cleared. He recognized Thornberg, Sherman, Doctor Pollock and Harry Farnham among the group. Another man who was familiar to him—probably from the lynch mob in the clearing. Three others he didn't know.

In front of them his gelding was still tethered to the hitching rail. Alongside, another horse that probably belonged to Wallace. As Reed veered around the animals, the big Noah Wallace lunged out of the saloon. Every man in the group bellowed an explanation to him, but Wallace ignored their voices and his face became dark with rage as he looked in the direction of their pointing arms.

"You bastard!" he roared, and drew the Remington from his hip holster.

Steele had moved nearer to the doorway, his legs feeling as weak as before but his punished mind no longer playing tricks with his vision.

He saw Wallace draw, heard male yells of approval and female screams of horror, blinked at the puff of smoke from the muzzle of the revolver, and cursed as the bullet dug up a spurt of dirt two feet in front of him.

When he squeezed the trigger of the rifle, it was as much an instinctive reaction as his earlier cleansing of the knife. A man was firing at him and the Virginian had developed a built-in response to such a situation. But his mind, working coolly amid the searing heat of pain, dictated where he aimed the bullet in a situation such as this.

It smashed into the lintel above the saloon doorway and dropped splinters down on the threshold. Reed and another man lunged inside the building. The rest froze, except for Wallace, who leveled his revolver for a second shot.

The Virginian's gun exploded first, the aim altered to send the bullet cracking within an inch of the blacksmith's temple and then through the window of the saloon. Wallace roared an obscenity as he ducked and spoiled his aim. Then he joined the others in whirling to spurt for the safety of the building's interior.

Steele went forward, leaping across the inert form of Boyd, to reach the door. It opened outwards, and he was dangerously exposed for a moment as he dragged it closed, slamming it against its twin. A bullet thudded into the timber, but did not penetrate. He cracked it open just an inch or so, then sank gratefully down on his haunches.

The exertion had created fresh waves of pain under his skull and it was difficult to separate the imagined sounds within his head from those outside. Then his mind cleared. Men were shouting, women were shrieking and footfalls were thudding—against hard-packed dirt and raised sidewalks. Until the voice of Wallace cut across all the other noise, and ended it.

"Steele, you hear me, Steele?" There was a brief pause and, for the first time since he had come to Fairoaks, the Virginian heard the cool-sounding splash of the stream water crossing the street beneath the wooden bridge. "All right, I know you can hear me," Wallace continued. "We all seen Marvin Boyd lying in there with his throat cut. And Oscar Reed got close enough to see he ain't never gonna get up from there until he's carried."

A woman sobbed.

A man cursed.

"Same way there ain't no escape from there for you, Steele. Now we ain't gun-totin' people, Steele. But we can use them if we have to. We got them now and we got you covered. So you better come out—holdin' that fancy rifle of yours high up above your head. You do like I'm sayin' and just maybe we'll hear what you got to say—and hold you for when Jesse Cutler gets back to town. You don't, we gonna rush you, Steele. And if you ain't dead already, you'll get the same as the Ford kid."

This time the pause was marked only by the babbling of the stream. The sound of water served to emphasize the arid dryness that unconsciousness had left in Steele's throat.

"Answer me, mister!" Wallace snarled.

The Virginian ejected the two spent shell cases from the rifle and loaded fresh rounds into the chambers.

"Not going to say yes and not going to say no, feller!" he yelled.

"What the—"

"Because I don't like the way you said maybe," Steele cut in.

"Where's Abigail?" Harvey Grover rasped. From behind and above Steele.

The Virginian stayed on his haunches as he turned, and looked once more at the aimed Winchesters of the Grover brothers. Both of the men were crouched at the edge of the hayloft from where Steele's attacker—and Boyd's killer—had swung the pitchfork.

"She went on through toward the Ford place," he answered, and nodded toward the corpse. "I didn't kill him."

"You had no reason I know of," Harvey allowed.

Leroy seemed unconvinced of this.

Steele took off his hat and turned the back of his head toward them. He had already felt the congealed blood coating the swelling where the pitchfork had broken over his skull.

"You sure couldn't have done that yourself," Harvey said.

"But maybe Marv did it before Steele killed him," Leroy growled.

"That's a pretty lousy maybe as well," Steele countered as he replaced his hat.

Then dived to the floor as a fusillade of shots thudded bullets into the double doors. Some were imbedded in the timbers. Others, from rifles, penetrated to thud into stall fronts and the battered desk.

"Best you come up here, Mr. Steele," Harvey offered, and put down his rifle to reach out both hands.

Leroy followed his example.

"Give you a minute to make up your mind, Steele!" Wallace roared. "Then we're gonna come in and get you."

"'Less you come out first!" Thornberg added.

By the time the telegraph operator had made his comment, Steele was up in the hayloft. Harvey had taken the Colt Hartford and Leroy had raised the Virginian clear of the floor with as much ease as if he had been a loosely packed bag of straw.

The door into the loft was still open and Steele went across to peer outside as soon as Harvey had handed him back his rifle.

"You goin' to make a run for it," the elder brother asked, keeping his voice low.

From the opening at the top of the outside stairway, the Virginian could see almost the whole length of the western stretch of Fairoaks's main street; and along the spur trail to where it plunged into the shade of the high timber. The street was empty, but the trail was peopled with men in work clothes and young children. All of them heading home from work and school for the midday meal, and abruptly hurrying after hearing the volley of shots. He could not see the Grovers' horses.

"No chance," he answered, and raked his dark eyes along the steep slope of the loft's street-facing roof. But it was weather-sealed with pitch between the timbers and there were no cracks or knot holes. So he went down onto his haunches and leaned his back against the side wall, a couple of feet to the left of the opening. "You declare it a holiday at the farm?" he asked a little wearily.

"You better make up your mind, Steele!" Thornberg yelled.

The demand increased Leroy's nervousness, but Harvey ignored it to the same extent as Steele.

"Got to thinkin' we only had your word for most of what happened, Mr. Steele. Seein' as how Abigail was out cold most of the time. Me and Leroy both took to you last night and early this mornin'. But, after you'd gone off with our sister, Leroy reminded me what I said about you not bein' the helpin' kind unless there was somethin' in it for you."

"Hold it, Noah!" John Sherman yelled. "People comin' down the north trail."

"Damn!" Wallace snarled.

"Warm light of day?" the Virginian drawled wryly, as he wiped sweat from his forehead with the back of a gloved hand. It was much hotter in the loft than down in the livery.

Outside, more shouts were exchanged. The homecoming workers and children demanding to know what had happened and those who knew urging them to get clear of the Wallace premises.

"I guess so," Harvey answered. "Rode on the

trail to where you were ambushed. Found the slugs in the trees. And some you fired. Lots of empty shell cases. Blood on the patrol track, like you said."

"Patrol track?"

"There's a whole mess of them, all over," Leroy supplied. "High summers and droughts, always a danger of forest fires. So folks around here take turns to ride the timber. Make sure none start."

Steele nodded, as the noise outside became less, the newcomers getting the message about the danger and hurrying into cover.

"Blood led you nowhere?"

"You knew it wouldn't?"

"To a dead horse, maybe. Or the feller saw his mount was bleeding and put a stop to it."

Harvey shook his head. "No dead horse. But the blood ran out a quarter mile from where it started. No sign we could see that showed if he rode back into town on the patrol track or took one of the side spurs. We'd seen enough, though. So we just came on into town on the track and heard the ruckus."

"Came up here in case you had Abigail with you," Leroy added. "But, seein' as how you ain't, I reckon we'll—"

"You had more than a minute, Steele!" Wallace snarled at the end of a brief silence from outside. "We're comin', and we got us a rope!"

". . . Have to sit it out, Leroy," Harvey growled, putting a different ending to the sentence his brother had started.

But nobody heard it, for his words were totally masked by a new fusillade of shots and courage-inspiring battle cries. Once more, some bullets came to a thudding halt in the door while others smashed through to bury themselves in the interior woodwork of the livery. Running feet thudded against the street surface. The initial volley became a constant barrage and individual slugs joined in a relentless effort to tear great holes in the double doors.

Leroy Grover scrambled to the rear of the hayloft. His brother withdrew to comparative safety in less haste.

Steele drew himself erect against the wall, leaving his rifle on the floor. His burnished, lined face expressed nothing of what he felt as he inched closer to the opening, one gloved hand rising to fist around a weighted corner of the thuggee scarf.

The Grovers did not see the thin figure of Herman Thornberg until he reached the top of the stairway and plunged through the opening into the hayloft, at the same instant that the double doors below were flung wide to admit the breathless attackers.

Steele had heard the man's running feet on the stairway treads. But didn't know who was making the flank approach until Thornberg rushed into the loft, and was pulled up short by the sight of Harvey and Leroy crouched in front of haybales stacked against the slope of the loft's rear roof. Instinctively, as the men below came silent as they peered at the empty livery, the skinny telegraph operator swung his Colt revolver toward the brothers.

The Virginian's right hand wrenched forward, drawing the scarf from around his neck. Then he changed the movement to a whip action, to curl the length of material in front of Thornberg's throat.

"Not us, Herman," Harvey Grover said calmly, and leveled his Winchester in case Thornberg was panicked into making a wrong shot.

It had only been necessary for Steele to take one step to bring his victim into range. As Thornberg vented a cry of terror at the touch of the scarf on his throat, Steele brought up his left hand, under the wrist of his right. His splayed fingers fisted around the flying, free end of the scarf and he locked his elbows together. Then turned away from the wall and stepped backward.

Thornberg's cry became a choked scream, curtailed almost immediately as Steele exerted more pressure across the man's windpipe. His gun fell to the floor as he reached both clawed hands to try to hook them over the scarf. Steele's backward movement forced him to sit down heavily on his rump.

"Herman!" Wallace roared, silencing the shrill-voiced sounds of concern and fear vented by the other men below.

"He's too choked up to talk right now," Steele answered evenly, then grunted with exertion as he turned again, and backed to the edge of the hayloft—dragging his prisoner by the scarf-trapped neck.

"Holy cow!" Sherman rasped.

"Sonofabitch!" from Farnham.

"Oh, dear God!" muttered Reed.

Others simply gasped or stared with gaping mouths, all of them tracking their rifles and handguns up toward the loft. But fingers were eased away from triggers, for Steele was exposed to a hail of bullets for only a moment, during which shock and surprise froze his would-be killers. Then, a final yank on the scarf, and a shove with his knee, gave him some protection. For it caused the purple-faced, bulging-eyed, gaping-mouthed Thornberg to sit on the edge of the loft, his legs dangling in midair. Then, as Steele crouched behind his prisoner, he eased the tension in the scarf, just enough to allow Thornberg to breathe. The telegraph operator, aware he could not escape the stranglehold of the scarf, dropped his hands to grip the edge of the hayloft.

"Steele, you better . . . what the hell?"

Menace was replaced by shock in the voice and face of Noah Wallace as the Grover brothers moved into view, standing erect and flanking the captor and captive.

"Came to check Abigail, was all, Noah," Harvey said flatly. "Me and Leroy ain't no part of this."

It took Wallace a few moments to find his voice, as the dozen or so men around him divided their attention between the murdered Marvin Boyd and the quartet of men above them.

"You'll be a part of it!" he snarled at length. "As guilty as Steele if you don't try to stop him gettin' away. Same as helpin' him, that is."

There were nods of agreement, as the bullet-shattered doorway of the livery began to fill with a curious crowd—men, women and children.

"No way I can escape, feller," Steele admitted. "Unless you folks are reasonable enough to listen to me."

"So leave Herman be, Steele, and then we'll talk," Oscar Reed offered.

He seemed unaware that his hands were toying nervously with a lariat.

The Virginian directed a cold grin toward the barber with the sweat-sheened bald head. "I said listen, feller. And Herman and me would both be grateful if you'd get rid of that rope. Don't need reminding what we both got hanging over us."

Reed dropped the lariat with a start and a small cry, as if the rope had suddenly become too hot to handle.

"The Grovers can blast him before he gets a chance to—" the freckle-faced Sherman started.

"Nothin' doin', Noah," Harvey growled.

"I'm with my brother," Leroy added.

"Send someone else around the side, Noah," the blond, squint-eyed Harry Farnham suggested.

"You want to comment on that, feller?" Steele said softly, his mouth close to Thornberg's ear. He eased the tension of the scarf.

"No!" the telegraph operator croaked. "He'll kill me for sure! Please, Noah! Hear him out!"

Steele tugged on both ends of the scarf. Just enough to cut off further words without interrupting Thornberg's pained breathing.

"Heard this town protects its own?"

Wallace shrugged and the fires went out in his pale-blue eyes. A few other men sighed. Out on the street, the large crowd became tense.

"So talk, Steele," the blacksmith invited. "Convince us it wasn't your knife opened Marv Boyd's throat. But it better be good. On account you're a couple of shakes away from murderin' another citizen of this town."

98

The Virginian felt a stirring of doubt in the back of his mind. Wallace's turnabout had been too fast and too easy. And some men and women had reacted even before the big man with the squashed nose had submitted to the demand. Steele raked his dark eyes over the faces of the watchers below him. Then glanced up at Leroy standing on his left. The shorter, duller-faced Grover brother looked more nervous than ever. As he started to swing his head to look at Harvey, Steele froze. And his insides seemed to turn to ice, even though the gun muzzle pressed into the nape of his neck felt searingly hot.

"Name's Cutler, mister," a gravel-voiced man growled. "Lawman in this part of the country."

Grins of triumph spread across some of the sweating faces below. Others continued to express sympathy—doubtless for Thornberg—and fear.

"Don't know what's happenin' here, but intend to find out. Whether over your dead body or not is up to you."

"Saw him comin', Mr. Steele," Harvey admitted evenly. "Me and Leroy can't go up against the law."

"You got any here?" Steele answered evenly. "Apart from not allowing whores in town?"

"Sheriff Cutler'll give you a fair hearin'," Harvey answered.

"Ain't nothin' you can do but throw in the towel, Steele," Wallace crowed. "Jesse can blow your head off before you got a chance to harm Herman."

"Listen to what the man tells you, mister!" the sheriff urged in his gruff voice.

"In the event you don't get a fair hearin', Mr. Steele," Harvey went on. "Leroy and me'll—"

"You done enough!" Wallace cut in angrily. "Stay out of this or get what's comin' to Steele!"

The Virginian released the scarf with his left hand and pulled it away from Thornberg's neck with the right. As Steele rose from the crouch and the released man began to massage his punished neck, many guns were tracked onto the target again, and fingers curled around triggers. Cutler had risen with Steele, to keep the revolver muzzle pressed against his flesh. To either side, first Harvey and then Leroy canted their Winchesters down into the livery, swinging the barrels back and forth.

Outside on the street, women hugged hungry children close to them. Men come home for the midday meal licked their lips nervously and mopped at their sweating brows, not relishing the tension that seemed to double the heat of the sun.

"You Grover boys been warned!" Oscar Reed snarled.

Steele showed his even, very white teeth in a harsh grin. His tone of voice was as flat as the dark pools of his eyes. "Seems like it could get to be quite a lynch hour."

CHAPTER EIGHT

Jesse Cutler was the same height as Steele but probably weighed twice as much as the compactly built, lean Virginian. He had a fleshy face with skin the color and texture of old and ill-used rawhide, the puffed cheeks threatening to engulf the small nose and close the tiny, flint-gray eyes. His chin was a series of curved steps below his thicklipped mouth. He had no waist, except where it was marked by his single-holster gunbelt, over the front of which his stomach drooped like a partially deflated balloon. He was dressed in a white shirt and tie, black vest, suit pants and derby hat, the incomplete outfit sweat-stained and grubby after the long trip back from his appearance at the Jamestown circuit court. He was not wearing a badge of office.

Steele saw all this as the gun was removed from the nape of his neck and he turned to look at the backstepping lawman. This put his own back toward the men below, but the Grover brothers continued to cover the potential lynch mob.

"Why is he such a buddy of yours, Harvey?" Sherman demanded, his tone sneering.

"Yeah, what makes you think so highly of him to risk your necks?" Farnham augmented.

"We just think," the elder brother answered evenly. "Some folks do that only after they acted."

During this brief exchange, the Virginian and the lawman surveyed each other, seeing the outer shell of the opposing man's face and drawing first impressions of what lay beneath. Steele thought he read a determined stubborn streak in Cutler.

"You men down there!" the lawman croaked. "I'm takin' this feller over to my place. And I don't want no interference. Noah, you come along. Some of you others give Doc Pollock a hand to move the remains of Marv."

He gestured with his Tranter for Steele to move ahead of him toward the opening onto the stairway.

"We're comin', too, sheriff," Harvey Grover insisted, against a complaining mumble of voices from below.

"Sure you are," Cutler replied, and there was a melancholic tone in his croaky voice, matched by a look in his flesh-squeezed eyes. "Something down there for you to see. And you won't like it."

"Watch him, Jesse!" Wallace called. "He carries a knife in his boot."

Cutler told Leroy to get the knife and weighted scarf. Harvey, anxiously puzzled by the lawman's cryptic comment, picked up the Colt Hartford. Then all four men descended the outside stairway, moved off the spur trail and swung right onto the western stretch of the street.

The crowd had broken up, many of the company workers, women and children going into their homes. A knot of people surrounded the men carrying the corpse to the doctor's house. Noah Wallace joined the group behind Steele and a few men stood and watched until the prisoner and his escorts went from sight.

Like Pollock, Jesse Cutler worked from his home which was one of the smaller houses on the north side of the street, midway between the bridge and the western limit of Fairoaks. A shingle on the wall beside the front door announced his name and line of business. His garden was one of the less well tended ones and his house was shabby with neglected paintwork.

As he was urged along the path toward the porch, Steele saw that one of the front windows had stout bars outside the glass. The parlor smelled musty from being closed up and unoccupied during the period Cutler was out of town. It was dusty and untidy, overcrowded with furniture, half of it suited to a living room and the rest designed for office use. One of the three doors leading off had another door in front of it—made up of iron bars.

"Well, sheriff?" Harvey demanded tautly when all the men were inside, with the front door closed.

Cutler waved his gun to order Steele onto a straight-backed chair beside a desk backed against a wall. "Sorry, Harvey . . . Leroy. On my horse out back. It's Abigail. She's dead, boys."

Tears spilled from Leroy's eyes immediately. Harvey vented a choked sob, then lunged across the room, banging into furniture. His brother trailed him closely and both crashed open a door to one side of the fireplace. As he sat down, Steele saw the door gave onto a kitchen. Another one was opened and the Grovers could no longer be heard as they lunged out into the yard.

"How, Jesse?" Wallace demanded from out of deep shock. "Where?"

"Strangled," the lawman answered, as he sank wearily into a padded swivel chair facing the desk, then swung it to look and point his Tranter at Steele. "I'd say with hands, rather than some fancy kerchief. A mile out along the west trail between the Smith and Ford places. Strangled and dumped in the ditch."

"Soon won't be any folks left around here at this rate," Wallace growled, glowering at Steele.

"I saw what happened to Marv," Cutler answered, showing the same degree of distaste for the silent, implacable Virginian.

Wallace swallowed hard. "Not only him, Jesse." He lowered his voice. "Marty was killed yesterday."

There was a moment, while the lawman was suffering shock at the revelation, when Steele knew he could take Cutler. But Wallace was wise enough to recognize the danger, and draped a hand over the butt of his holstered Remington when Cutler's gaze swung toward him.

"And Emmet Ford," the Virginian put in evenly, pensively eyeing his rifle, knife and scarf which lay on a small, two-place dining table.

"Hold on!" Cutler croaked, covering Steele with his gun and his gaze again. "Marty Fuller's dead? That's terrible! Let me get this straight. Why the hell didn't you telegraph me in Jamestown? Let me hear this from the beginnin', Noah."

Wallace cleared his throat to start the report, and seemed a little nervous. Steele guessed this was because the blacksmith did not expect the news of the lynching to be well received. But then he was given a respite, as the Grover brothers crossed the kitchen and entered the main room of the house. Leroy held the limp form of the mourning-garbed Abby in his arms, her head draped with Cutler's suit jacket. The sheriff's badge of office was pinned to the left lapel. Harvey carried both Winchesters. Tears had dried on their faces.

"Ain't fittin' Abigail should stay on a horse out in the yard," Harvey said to Cutler. "Leroy'll take her down to Doc Pollock's place."

The lawman nodded, grave-faced. "Sure, boys. Sorry I had to leave her there. But, what with the shootin' at Noah's place, I figured I had more pressin' business with the livin'."

Leroy took his sister out through the front door. Harvey asked where she had been found and Cutler told him, adding that the woman's pinto mare was nowhere around. Then Harvey sat at the small table and looked imploringly at the Virginian.

"What do you think, Mr. Steele? Why'd it happen?"

"Hold on there!" Cutler croaked. "We'll get to Abby, Harvey. But it seems I got some other killin's to catch up on."

Inevitably, the elder Grover brother was concerned only with the murder of Abby. But Steele spoke before Harvey could voice the obvious.

"I've got other things on my mind right now, feller."

Cutler was intrigued, and a little irritated, by the relationship between Grover and Steele—which seemed to place him on the outside.

"Yeah, that's right. You have, Mr. Steele." Harvey slumped low on the chair and lost himself in his own thoughts.

Wallace wore an expression of his own brand of misery as he began to relate the events of yesterday and this morning. Steele listened as attentively as the lawman, seeking to discover discrepancies or learn additional information. But the morose blacksmith did not deviate from the facts as far as Steele knew them. And offered nothing fresh until he revealed he had spent most of this morning at the timber company base camp where he had a forge.

Cutler scowled his anger at news of the lynching, and urged Wallace to get on when the blacksmith started to repeat the amount of evidence against Emmet Ford. Then, when the report was completed, just as Leroy Grover returned, the lawman said: "You should have locked him up and telegraphed me."

With his story done, Wallace seemed physically unburdened. And was able to meet low-keyed anger with an identical emotion. "Ain't a single man in this town would've waited, Jesse! We had the Ford boy dead to rights and weren't no way to control the folks here. Not with Marty Fuller lyin' dead."

Cutler waved away the excuse. "Your turn now, mister!" he snapped at Steele. "First, why you're in this part of the country. Then how it happened Marvin Boyd got killed to rouse up the local people again."

The Virginian complied, watching both Wallace and Cutler closely, but without appearing to be anything but indifferent to his situation. The lawman continued to burn with low-key anger, but it was not directed toward Steele. As the blacksmith heard about last night's shootings and the events of the morning he became morose again—perhaps as a shield for something else.

"Leroy and me checked out on the trail, sheriff," Harvey said to end a silence which followed the conclusion of Steele's account. "There are bullets and blood, just like he said there was."

"Let's see where you claimed to have got hit, mister!" Cutler demanded.

Steele removed his hat and turned his head.

"You sure enough got hit," the lawman allowed.

"And there's a pitchfork busted in two at my place," Wallace added quickly. His burnished face seemed almost pallid as he met Steele's blankeyed stare after the Virginian had replaced the hat gingerly on his aching head.

"I saw it, Noah," Cutler said, and slid the Tranter into his holster. Then he swung the chair to glare at Wallace. "Makes you feel kinda weak at the knees, I guess. Knowin' you almost lynched this guy?"

The challenge raised Wallace's anger again. "It wasn't just me, Jesse." He stood up fast and now his eyes were glowering as he stared at Steele. "And anyway, there ain't no proof he didn't cut Marv's throat."

"Ain't no proof he did. And you only had

107

circumstantial evidence against the Ford boy."
Cutler's voice was calm.

Wallace's temper rose. "What you gonna do, Jesse?" he demanded. "Arrest the whole damn town? Only ten of us went after him, but the whole damn town was behind us."

"No, Noah. Gonna investigate this whole mess the law's way. Way it should have been from the start. And if it turns out Ford didn't blast Marty, then I'll have to put my mind to what to do about the lynchin'. The boy been buried yet?"

The blacksmith controlled his temper. But his voice was throaty with the strain. "No. We figured to plant him out in the timber. Unmarked."

"Be nice if you and some of the other lynchers took him out to his place and buried him, Noah. Some kind of atonement in the event he didn't kill Marty Fuller. And even if he did, you still done the wrong thing."

Wallace seemed on the point of refusing. But then he growled, whirled, and stormed out of the house.

"Am I free to leave, sheriff?" Steele asked.

"This house, sure. But stay close to town, mister. You Southerners are strong on your word of honor, I hear?"

Steele stood up, and his vision went haywire again as his head pounded, the injury complaining at the need of the man to move after a long period of welcome rest. But it lasted only a few moments. "You've got it, feller" he said with a bleak smile. "And I'm not about to break my word after somebody tried to break my head."

The tiny eyes of the fat-faced sheriff were lit with a grim light as he watched the Virginian replace his knife and scarf and pick up the Colt Hartford.

"The folks around here know damn well I won't do nothin' about them takin' the law into their own hands, Steele!" he croaked. "But a stranger won't get off so light."

"I'm ready to respect the law," Steele replied evenly as he moved to the door. "If it's what it should be."

"I do a good job around here, mister! These killin's will get investigated. Just like I told Noah Wallace they would. And I don't want no interference."

"Won't get in your way, sheriff."

He pulled open the door and stepped out into the overgrown garden of the house.

"Where'll you be, Mr. Steele?" Harvey Grover called after him.

"Eating, feller," the Virginian answered, and closed the door.

The cooking fires were out now and their smoke was a just perceptible taint on the hot air of early afternoon. The timber workers had returned to their jobs and the children had gone back to school. The single street of the pleasant little town was totally deserted except for Adam Steele and his horse.

Birds chirped in the trees and the stream gurgled and bubbled. As he reached the front of the saloon where the gelding was hitched, the steam machinery at the timber company sawmill began to thud. He had sensed watching eyes of women in the houses. But nobody looked out at him from the plate glass windows of the business premises. The bullet-scarred double doors of the livery were both firmly closed. So was the hatchway into the hayloft above.

As Steele unfastened one of his saddlebags and lifted down a canteen, a wagon started to move. Along at the eastern end of Fairoaks. He led his horse into the shade of the oak and allowed the animal to drink from the stream where it emerged from under the bridge. Then hitched the reins to a low branch.

By that time, a two-horse team had hauled a flatbed wagon out onto the street from the back lot of the doctor's house. Noah Wallace drove and the priest, Menken, sat on the seat beside him— garbed in cleric's black with a clean white collar. Riding on the back were the other men who had formed the lynch mob of yesterday—minus, of course, Marvin Boyd.

Resentment was almost a palpable emanation from the men aboard the wagon as it clattered slowly across the bridge timbers and then rolled along the western stretch of the street. Every pair of eyes bore a glare into the unresponsive face of the Virginian.

The tailgate of the wagon was down and Steele saw the plain pine coffin it carried, acting as a seat to a few of the reluctant burial detail.

"We ain't so easy to get took in as Jesse Cutler, mister!" the redheaded Harry Farnham snarled.

"So you better not try to leave Fairoaks!" John Sherman warned. He dropped a hand to drape the butt of a holstered Colt.

Steele saw that several other men had armed themselves. And that Oscar Reed was again toying with a length of rope—that would probably be needed to lower the coffin into the grave. But

110

the barber's meaningful stare implied it could be put to another use.

The Virginian glanced up and down the single street of the appropriately named town set in the forest of towering trees.

"Grateful for the warning," he drawled after the departing wagon. "But it's not needed. It has to be somebody else's funeral before I'm out of the woods."

CHAPTER NINE

The saloon doors were still fastened open, but Steele remained in the shade of the tree on the stream bank. He ate a cold meal from his supplies and washed it down with water from the stream, then filled his canteen. Around him, the town stayed quiet and the street was not disturbed by movement until Harvey and Leroy Grover emerged from the lawman's house.

The brothers were grim-faced and their pace was funereal. Leroy turned on the spur trail and Harvey crossed to join Steele in the shade of the tree.

"Tethered our horses in the timber," the elder brother said absently as he leaned his back against the trunk of the oak. "Leroy's gone to get them. How's your head?"

"It feels like a pitchfork was broken over it," Steele growled. "If you care."

Harvey shrugged off his preoccupation and included Steele in the matters concerning him. "Talkin' to keep from blowin' my stack."

"At Cutler?"

"Figures to sweep the mess under the carpet," Harvey answered, staring morosely down at the fast-running stream, sparkling with dappled sunlight.

"He's just going to let it lay?"

A shake of the head. "He'll make some kinda effort, for the sake of appearances. But he's already made up his mind what happened. Says Martin Fuller was killed by Ford and a passin' stranger. Abigail saw what happened and got killed by the stranger to stop her tellin' it."

Leroy led the two horses across the street. As Steele glanced up at him, he saw another man, farther down the street. Sheriff Cutler, standing in the doorway of his house, watching for a reaction from the Virginian. Then, as soon as he saw he had been spotted, the lawman withdrew inside and closed the door.

"Gonna follow that line of investigation, he says," Harvey continued. "But reckons the stranger's long gone by now."

"He tell you to tell me this?" the Virginian rasped between clenched teeth.

Harvey met Steele's abruptly angry eyes and was perplexed by the change of mood. "Yeah."

"Also said to tell you there ain't no need to stay in town, Mr. Steele," Leroy added. "On account of there's nothin' more you can help him with."

"Grateful for the message," Steele said, as he unhitched the reins of the gelding from the branch and swung up into the saddle.

"You leavin'?" Harvey asked, surprised and disappointed.

He received a nod in response. Then: "But I reckon I'll be back."

He jerked on the reins to turn the horse, then heeled him across the street and onto the spur

113

trail. The cold light of anger continued to burn in his dark eyes and his gentle mouthline was slightly twisted—to give his expression a quality of bitterness and, perhaps, evil.

Beyond the rear of the livery and blacksmith's forge, he entered the high timber, then swung right, onto one of the fire-patrol tracks. It had been a fast departure from town, but the speed was not dictated by anger. Rather, by a clearly thought-out decision to take a calculated risk.

Perhaps the sheriff of Fairoaks was as crafty and lazy as he looked. Or perhaps he genuinely believed he had come up with a possible solution. Whichever, it could be made to fit the facts and—the cause of Steele's anger—he fitted into the vacant slot as the passing stranger.

He slowed the gelding to an easy walk and as the sweat began to dry on his face, he felt the anger drain out of him.

A falling out of thieves had led to Emmet Ford being handed over to the lynch mob. Ford's girl had to be silenced, perhaps because she had demanded a share of the money taken from Fuller's safe—and had been strung along with promises until a suitable opportunity occurred. Marvin Boyd had witnessed the latest killing and had himself been killed because of it.

As a theory, it had more holes than the double doors of the livery stable. But who in Fairoaks would question it? When it let the lynchers off the hook and allowed Cutler to ignore their brutal act. And made the surviving guilty party a stranger among the tight-knit citizens of the town.

All that it needed to patch over the holes was

114

for Steele to leave town—and for Cutler to condone the formation of another lynch mob. A group of men who would act without thought, then put the whole sorry mess out of their minds as the lynch town returned to being a quiet, pleasant community again.

Steele did not have to ride all the way to where the rifleman had waited last night. For he found the point on the narrow track where the wounded horse had stopped marking its course with splashes of blood. When he dismounted and started back the way he had come, there were plenty of signs to be seen but the very quantity made for difficulty in tracking. A man had ridden over this part of the forest floor last night. Today, the Grovers had passed over the same route. And Steele himself had steered his gelding in the opposite direction along the track.

But, almost half a mile from where the ambusher had fired at him, he found a side track where the man had veered his injured mount. It had taken Steele more than an hour to cover this much ground, for many tracks cut away from the east-west one and he explored deep along each of them before abandoning them. All the time, he listened for sounds that might indicate he was being hunted in the timber. He heard none.

Then, as he made faster progress along the track that meandered northward through the redwoods—following just one set of signs—he was struck by the possibility of a variation to the scheme of Sheriff Cutler. Perhaps the lawman intended to delay pursuit so that Steele—running scared—would be sure to escape capture. The citizens of Fairoaks would suffer bitter frustration—but there would be no risk of Steele being able to reason his way free of guilt.

Although this forest was in California, it was only the towering height of the giant redwoods that made it any different from similar country in the eastern states. Country over which Steele had fought a vicious and bloody war; often in full-scale battles, but more frequently as part of a small group reconnoitering Federal positions and movements. So he was no stranger to the art of tracking over such terrain.

When he found what he was looking for, he was within earshot of the machinery at the timber company sawmill. It was in another clearing, much smaller than the one where Emmet Ford had been hanged. Manmade by the felling of trees, with an iron tank filled with water and a rack of beating tools for use in fighting fires.

It was unlikely the sniper would have selected the spot by choice, but it was here that his horse had collapsed, perhaps in exhaustion or maybe in death. It was impossible to see where Steele's bullet had wounded the animal or if any other injury had been inflicted. Equally impossible to see what color the animal had been or whether it was male or female.

For the carcass had been cremated. It was on its side, legs stretched out at right angles from the hind and forequarters. Brush had been stuffed beneath it and piled around and on top of it. A great deal of brush, that was now just gray ash; its light shade giving starkness to the black, roasted flesh of the carcass.

As if the gelding sensed it was one of its own kind that had died here, the horse scraped restlessly at the ground where Steele had hitched him to the rack of fire-fighting tools.

Crouched at the side of the remains, his nostrils wrinkled against the smell of old burning and cooked meat beginning to putrefy, Steele decided he could learn nothing more than the obvious fact that was before his eyes. And that the chance he could find and follow the sign of a man on foot was too long to be even considered.

But perhaps the horse carcass and the effective way in which identifying marks had been obliterated was enough for the time being. Certainly it was more convincing proof of the truth of his story than the bullets and shell cases close to the east trail. Enough to cause some of the citizens of Fairoaks to doubt Cutler's theory?

He sighed as he stood up, then moved to the water storage tank. He took off his hat and plunged his aching head into the tepid water. It had a soothing effect as it washed away the crusting of blood from the split bruise. And, when he surfaced, he found he could think more clearly. The disturbed water calmed, then began to move with gentle ripples as drops splashed down from his hair. The reflection of his face was by turns clear and convoluted. And he saw the changing images as a mirror of his actions since he first became involved with the people of Fairoaks in another clearing.

Sometimes brutally selfish—totally in character with the kind of man he had become, as he sought to protect his life and his possessions. As when he had hurled the knife at Emmet Ford and then watched without compassion while the boy was lynched. Again when he had struck Abby Grover,

117

then when he had been determined not to die without taking the life of Herman Thornberg in return.

At other times his actions and the reasons for them were derived from the man he once had been. A man with a conscience who could feel an affinity to and sympathy for his fellow human beings. A man unwilling to take the easy way out and turn his back on an injustice—even though there was no reward for putting his life on the line. Short of the knowledge that a town of strangers would no longer consider him to be a murderer.

The kind of man Adam Steele had become did not normally give a damn about what people thought of him.

The gelding snorted—and another horse responded. Steele whirled and the sudden movement caused a hundred droplets of water to rain down onto the surface of the tank. But there was only the image of the high sun to be disturbed as he powered down into a crouch, streaking a hand into the gaping split of his pants leg.

"Only Leroy and me, Mr. Steele," Harvey Grover announced calmly. But his hand started to move toward the jutting stock of the Winchester in the rifle boot.

The Virginian had fisted a hand around the knife. Now he released it, and straightened slowly, picking up his fallen hat and replacing it on his wet head.

"Guess we know why you're so edgy," the younger brother said.

They were walking, leading their mounts by

the reins, Harvey in front as they emerged from the patrol track into the clearing.

"After you left town, Jesse Cutler looked real pleased," Harvey said. "Said he figured you would—if you was the passin' stranger."

"He send you out to look for me?" Steele asked, moving out of the way as the Grovers brought their horses to the tank to drink.

Harvey shook his head.

Leroy spat. "Said he'd had a long ride and he'd sleep on the idea, Mr. Steele. Harvey figured we ought to check on what you were up to."

They had left their horses and gone to the other side of the clearing to examine the burned carcass. Steele had intended to go to the gelding, to be close to the Colt Hartford. But then he started to think clearly again, after the tautness of tension flooded out of him. The Grovers could have got the drop on him with ease, so their cool calmness now was not a part of a trick.

"You made a better job of tracking than earlier," he said, suddenly realizing why he had been acting out of character so often since Emmet Ford died.

"Just worried about Abigail then," Leroy replied as both brothers came erect beside the burned horse.

"Nothin' we can do to help her now," Harvey added. "Except find out who killed her and string him up the same way as Emmet Ford."

The Grovers were decent men. As were most others in Fairoaks and the surrounding timber country. A nice town in fine country, populated for the most part with honest kind, hard-working people. But people who would naturally get riled

119

up when something as evil as murder did more than cause a ripple on the calm surface of their smooth lives.

It was the kind of place, among the kind of people, where Adam Steele could try to put down new roots. Geographically far from his native Virginia, but in appearance as close as he was ever likely to get. But if a stranger hoped to be accepted by such people in such a place, he had to show he was as one with them. Not as they were now, uncharacteristically brutal in their burning desire to track down a vicious killer. Rather, just a normal human being: both good and evil but with the finer feelings more than counterbalancing the bad in all men.

"And you're sure I'm not the one you're looking for?" the Virginian asked.

Leroy spat and Harvey scowled. "Jesse Cutler could be a good lawman if he gave himself half a chance, Mr. Steele. He don't think you're the one, either. Though he won't admit it until he has to. It's just you're nice and handy to fit the bill. Saves him havin' to think too hard or do any work—which is somethin' he likes even worse."

"You have something in mind?"

Harvey shrugged. "Figure you're goin' to do the sheriff's work for him. Never could be easy. Hell of a lot harder if folks buy Jesse Cutler's idea of how things happen."

"And we got a very personal interest, Mr. Steele," Leroy pointed out.

His brother ignored the comment. "You shown you can handle yourself. But ain't no man was ever born that don't need some help sometime or other. You got any objection to me and Leroy takin' a piece of your action, Mr. Steele?"

"We ain't much in the brains department," Leroy admitted with a shrug. "But we can sure—"

"That's enough, Leroy," his brother advised. "Mr. Steele knows about us. We don't have to sell ourselves to him. Right, Mr. Steele?"

"You're not selling, feller," the Virginian said earnestly. "Buying—yourselves a lot of trouble, maybe."

Harvey shook his head. "Only thing that troubles me is that Abigail's killer might get off scot-free."

"And I sure as hell ain't scared of that bunch in town!" Leroy snapped.

Steele pursed his lips and let his breath run out noisily between them. "If you want to stick your necks out," he drawled, then showed his teeth in a grin that did not reach his eyes. "Just have to hope we don't end up as three very high-strung fellers."

CHAPTER TEN

Emmet Ford had been buried in front of the small house, at the center of the flower garden. In the digging of the grave and the filling in after the coffin was lowered into the ground, the reluctant and resentful burial detail had spared no thought for the colorful blooms. Just a few heads here and there were still held erect on untouched stalks. The rest had been trampled underfoot, scythed down by carelessly wielded shovels, or crushed with earth now returned to the hole or formed into the mound. There was no marker to name the remains rotting below.

Steele and the Grovers dismounted at the open gateway in the picket fence and led their horses through into the yard, hitching them to the flatbed wagon still parked in front of the barn.

"They wore armbands and sad faces, but none of that were for my boy," Rose Ford called from inside the small house. "And the preacher didn't say but one prayer. You fellers want some lemonade?"

She stepped out onto the porch, a seemingly much older and thinner version of the woman Steele had seen here yesterday. She still wore the dress of white and red gingham and the gray denim apron, but the clothing was no longer crisp and clean. Neither was her homely face. Her gray hair had become loosened from the bun and hung in a straggled mess around and across her dirt-streaked features. Her eyes were red-rimmed and dull and her mouth was twisted into a line of bitterness. She looked as if she had not slept at all during the long and lonely night, and was dirty and exhausted from countless heavy chores.

"Real kind of you, ma'am," Steele answered. "If it isn't any trouble."

Automatically, he drew the Colt Hartford as he moved away from the gelding to approach the porch.

"Didn't even put a cross on the grave," Rose Ford muttered.

"See what you can do about that, Leroy," Harvey said, and the younger Grover nodded enthusiastically.

He went into the barn while Harvey followed in the wake of the Virginian. Glancing around, at the yard and buildings, Steele saw evidence of the chores that had kept the woman so busy and made her so dirty. The house windows sparkled from polishing, there was not a speck of dust on the porch, the vegetable patch had been stripped of weeds and a new area of yard had been dug over. She had been just as industrious inside the parlor, and perhaps the entire house. Furniture had been rearranged and cleaned and the floor and walls had been scrubbed. The room smelled antiseptically fresh—to such an extent that the newcomers could pick up their own and each other's scents—resulting from the long, hot ride along the patrol tracks to the north and then west of Fairoaks. But only for a few moments. Then, as the woman sank into her rocking chair beside the cold range, their nostrils were assaulted by the much worse odor emanating from her body. Sleep was not the only bodily need Rose Ford had failed to stop for during her frantic efforts to improve her surroundings.

"Help yourselves, fellers," she invited, closing her eyes and interlocking her fingers in her lap as she began to rock the chair. "I won't join you. Can't allow sustenance to pass my lips. Penance for being a woman, like."

There were two glasses and a jug on the cloth-covered table, just as there had been yesterday. But they were empty and sparklingly clean.

"Grateful to you, Mrs. Ford," Steele replied evenly, sitting down on one side of the table and gesturing for the suddenly nervous Grover to use the other straight-backed chair.

"I was real worried all night when the man of the house didn't come home," the woman said, eyes still tightly closed as she rocked back and forth. Out in the barn, Leroy began to use a saw. "Kept busy, though, and that helped some. Don't think so many bad thoughts when I'm busy. About my boy chasin' after wicked women."

Harvey frowned at Steele, and the Virginian shook his head and held up a gloved hand to request silence.

"But he wasn't doin' that," the woman continued, her voice flat and empty of emotion. Tears began to run down her grimed face. "Was dead all the time. But it was that woman that led to it. I'm sure of that. He should have stayed home with me when his work was done. But no.

He wouldn't do that. Always chasin' after the kinda women that go with men."

"She's crazy," Steele hissed at the elder Grover as the man's face developed an angry scowl.

Mrs. Ford was still talking, her tone rising to a shrill shriek. And as the two men watched her, they saw that her face became abruptly contorted by a look of boundless hatred, her eyes snapping open to stare into infinity. She unlocked her hands and fisted them around the arms of the chair, rocking it violently.

"He was a good boy and it was women made him bad. The kind that go with men. The kind that open their womb to any man wants to get inside. And he was human, my boy. Just like his father. Ain't natural for men to say no to that kinda woman. Ain't no man can ever say no. And it don't never come to no good. A moment of evil pleasure of the flesh and a lifetime of trouble. It's always just like the good book says it'll be."

In the barn, Leroy was using a hammer now, but the woman's shrill voice and the creak of the rocker almost drowned all sounds from outside the small, clean and evil smelling room. As thoughts of the Bible entered her tormented mind, Mrs. Ford ended her tirade. She clasped her hands together again, but in an attitude of prayer, and became rock still except for her lips which formed silent words directed toward the ceiling and cloudless universe beyond.

"We're not goin' to get any sense out of her, Mr. Steele," Harvey growled, sending a venomous look toward the praying woman. "Nobody ever did."

"It's worth a try, feller," the Virginian an-

125

swered evenly, then raised his voice. "Mrs. Ford?"

She broke off from the prayer and looked toward the two men at the table. For a moment, she was surprised. Then she blinked and showed a coy smile. "Why, what are you boys doin' here in my house? Emmet comes home and finds you, I'll have some explainin' to do, I reckon. He don't like for me to entertain gentlemen callers when he's in town workin'. You want some lemonade?"

"What'd I tell you?" Harvey muttered.

Steele ignored him. "Have you had any other callers today, Mrs. Ford?" he asked.

"Why, mercy sakes, what kinda woman do you think I am, sir?" she demanded, throwing her hands to her filthy face. "I do not make a habit of servin' lemonade to all and sundry. I am as pure as the day I was born—in thought and deed."

"So how come you got a son, lady?" Harvey Grover snarled.

The smile vanished from the face of the crazy woman more suddenly than it had come. And she glared in harsh anger at the man who had forced the disturbing thought into her calm mind.

"You're one of them!" she shrieked. "One of them lyin', women-chasin' men that spreads rumors about me! Emmet was a virgin birth! On account you and your kind spend all your time tryin' to get into women's wombs, you think that can't happen! Well, it can. It happened like it's written in the good book. And it happened to me. So you get outta my house, mister! Take yourself and your dirty talk someplace else! If you don't do that right now, I'll have my boy run you off!"

She pushed herself upright from the chair and

126

swung to face the men at the table. Her hands and torso trembled with rage, but her feet were planted firmly on the floor and her stare did not waver as it poured scorn and hatred toward Steele and Grover.

"I ain't like other women! So ain't no use you comin' sniffin' around me! I'm decent and I'm raisin' my boy decent! Though Lord knows that's hard to do in a world this wicked!" Abruptly, she spat on the floor. "We're the only decent folks there is! All other women are whores and all other men are chasers of whores. And the whole bunch of you are damned to eternal life in the fires and brimstone of hell!"

"I ain't listenin' to no more of this, Steele!" Harvey growled, getting up so fast he knocked his chair over backward. Just for a moment, there was a glint of pity shining through his anger as he returned the woman's glare. Then he whirled and strode purposefully out of the house.

Steele stood up with less haste and canted the rifle casually to his shoulder. The woman's rage died and she lowered herself into the rocker.

"It don't matter about my boy no more," she said softly. "On account they buried him this mornin'. But it was Marty they was sad and wore black for." She sighed, and shifted her tear-gazed stare around the room. "Maybe if I clean the place up some, it'll help ease my mind."

"Abby Grover tell you what happened, ma'am?" Steele asked softly.

Mrs. Ford didn't raise her voice, but there was deep hatred in her eyes as they searched for and found the Virginian. "I might flirt with gentlemen callers, mister. But it's all in innocent fun.

But I don't have no truck with the kinda women that ain't no better than whores."

"I ain't stayin' to listen to that kinda talk about Abigail!" Harvey snarled from the porch. "I told you there's no sense to get out of her!"

"Good day, ma'am," Steele said, and touched the brim of his hat.

Rose Ford showed a sweet smile. "Been a pleasure talkin' with you, sir. I sure hope you enjoyed the lemonade?"

"It was fine," the Virginian said just before he stepped out into the afternoon sunlight blazing across the yard.

Harvey Grover had moved over to where the horses were hitched. Leroy was at the grave in the wrecked flower garden, admiring the neat cross he had made by nailing two pieces of unplaned timber together.

"Guess it should have his name on it, Mr. Steele," he called. "But I ain't learned much about spellin' so far."

"That's fine, Leroy," his brother assured. "At least the trip here wasn't altogether wasted."

Pleased with the mild praise, the younger brother straightened the cross where it was set at the head of the grave, and ambled across to the horses. "It was like you said it would be, uh, Harvey?"

"Yeah, Leroy."

"A man has to take the rough with the smooth," Steele said, swinging up into his saddle after sliding the Colt Hartford into the boot. "Knew she was as crazy as you said she was. But sometimes somebody like that can—"

"Hey, you fellers headin' into Fairoaks?" Rose

Ford called from the porch of the house, looking and sounding totally rational.

"Something we can do for you?" Steele answered.

"Certainly would appreciate it."

"Let's go," Harvey urged sullenly. "I've had more than I can take of her already."

"Had a horse stole," the woman called. "A roach-backed gray mare. Was in the stable last night and gone this mornin'. He won't stir his fat rump, but I'd appreciate it if you'd report the matter to Jesse Cutler."

Steele touched the brim of his hat again and heeled his horse forward to join the Grover brothers, who had ridden out through the open gateway.

Harvey glanced back toward the house, then spat. "Probably imagined the horse same as she dreams up most other things she talks about," he muttered.

The three of them moved along the trail together, the Grovers closing up to flank Steele after he had made it clear he was staying in the open on the way back to town.

"Or maybe she just imagined he was stolen," the Virginian replied after a long pause, during which his face was set in a pensive frown.

"She's ravin' mad, Mr. Steele," the elder brother growled. "Wasn't any sense in anythin' she said. Always has been that way. One minute actin' like a young girl with her cap set at any man happens to be handy; the next rantin' on about all the wickedness in the world."

"She say Abigail was no good again, Harvey?" Leroy asked.

"Yeah. And how she give birth to Emmet without no man touchin' her. Just like Abigail used to tell us she talked."

Leroy nodded sagely. "Guess she oughta be pitied, uh, Mr. Steele?"

The Virginian did not reply and the brothers became as silent as he was as they rode through the hot afternoon, the sinking sun thrusting their shadows out ahead of them. Steele continued to be thoughtful. Harvey was discontented, constantly shooting impatient glances toward the Virginian. Leroy was melancholy, perhaps thinking about the mad woman or, more likely, reflecting on the death of his sister.

As they rode on to the single street of Fairoaks, the distant sound of the steam machines at the sawmill indicated that the timber workers were still earning their daily dollars out in the forest to the north of town. But school was finished for the day, evidenced by children playing in gardens. Then, as the three riders advanced toward the center of town, mothers called for their offspring to go into the house. Those who were slow to respond suffered the indignity of being swept off their feet and carried inside, to the accompaniment of shrill-voiced scolding.

"Seems like we ain't welcome here," Leroy said.

"More Mr. Steele than you and me, Leroy," his brother corrected.

As they neared the center of town, Steele sensed watchful eyes behind windows. But only in the houses. The doors of the business premises were tightly closed and there was an empty feel to this section of Fairoaks. The slow clop of hooves on hard-packed, dusty dirt seemed to echo inside each building.

"I'm gonna have a beer," Harvey growled as he dismounted in front of the saloon. "It feels like I can taste what that crazy old woman smelled like."

"Make that two," Leroy said anxiously.

"I'll take care of my horse," Steele responded as the young Grover swung from the saddle and took care of hitching the animals—his brother already up on the sidewalk and pushing through the batwing doors.

The Virginian stayed mounted and veered the gelding across the street, not dropping to the ground until he was immediately outside the bullet-scarred doors of the livery. He pulled one of them open and led the horse into the shade of the stable.

There were six stalls occupied and he steered the gelding into an empty one. The broken pitchfork was still on the floor and he used the tined half to swing some feed into the stall box. Then he moved along the line of stalls, recognizing Menken's lame chestnut and four other horses that had been in the livery earlier. The newcomer was a roach-backed gray mare—the animal Wallace had ridden into town and hitched outside the saloon this morning.

"Rose Ford reckons you stole this horse, feller," the Virginian drawled evenly, and jerked up his head to look toward the hayloft.

The loft flooring creaked, and then the leather-aproned blacksmith came into view. The gunbelt was looped around his waist and his right hand was fisted on the butt of his Remington.

"She's crazy!"

"Most of the time," Steele allowed.

He had the pitchfork canted to his right shoulder, in the attitude he normally carried the Colt Hartford. But he had not intended it to be a weapon; he simply did not become aware of Wallace's presence until he was too far away from the rifle to have a hope of reaching it.

"It needs shoein'," the blacksmith growled. "She told me to bring him in and shoe him. Check his hooves, if you want."

"Believe you, feller," the Virginian answered. "That she asked you to work on him, too."

"So what's the beef, Steele?"

Steele pursed his lips. Then shrugged. "You're the one with the aimed gun, feller."

"Just me and Mr. Menken left in town, Steele. Apart from the women and children. Jesse Cutler's headin' up a posse out huntin' for you."

"Take a rope with them?"

A shake of the head. "No. They're all sworn-in deputies. It's a legal posse."

"That why you didn't go along?"

Another shake of the head. "Figured there was a chance you'd come back, Steele. I stayed around town in case you did."

"I did. You going to take another shot at me?"

Wallace licked his lips. He was standing on the edge of the loft, immediately above Steele, aiming the Remington down the length of his body and legs toward the upturned face of the Virginian.

"You should have done like Jesse thought you would, Steele."

"Run away from something I never did?"

"Been no skin off your nose. A man like you,

you could have lost a posse easy as wipin' your nose."

"I made a mistake, feller."

The leather-textured face of the blacksmith expressed confusion. "Mistake?"

A nod from Steele. "I thought I wanted to be part of this town. Or some other town like it. So I tried to handle things the way people in towns like this are supposed to. But people here are like people all over. Not all what they seem to be. So I've decided to be just me, feller."

"Don't try nothin', Steele!" Wallace warned, suddenly anxious. "I don't want to have to kill you."

"What do you want?"

"For you to get on your horse and ride out of this part of the country. But I guess you won't do that?"

"Reckon not, feller. That nose of mine you spoke of—I stuck it where it wasn't wanted. Maybe because I reckoned I could try to be something I'm not. But it's got a bad smell up it now. And what I am can't leave things this way."

He leaned slightly forward, so that his shoulder pushed the broken pitchfork onto a vertical line. Then he jerked his right hand upward—and lunged to the side. There was never a chance of the curled tines doing any damage to Wallace, for the move was by necessity telegraphed to the blacksmith. But it did startle the man, causing him to jerk backward as he instinctively squeezed the trigger of the Remington. The gun was off target and the bullet burrowed into the dirt, several feet away from where Steele had been standing.

The Virginian remained on his feet as he slammed into the side of an end stall. But went into a stoop, to gape the split in his pants leg and reach inside for the knife.

"I told you, Steele!" Wallace shrieked, and leaped down from the loft, turning himself in midair and tracking the Remington across the rear wall of the stable.

Using the flat of the sole of one foot against the stall to give him a powerful boost, Steele rocketed forward.

The Remington exploded another shot. Steele felt the rush of air and heat of burnt powder at the side of his head. Then his body, lunging forward, slammed into the downward moving form of Noah Wallace. The blacksmith rasped an obscenity and staggered in an ungainly reverse run, flailing his arms and trying to level his gun at Steele. The Virginian went with him, slashing just once with the knife. Wallace screamed and hurled away the Remington, his gun hand suddenly streaming arterial blood from a gash in the wrist.

The bigger man tripped then, and sprawled out on his back. Steele, a look of ice-cold rage carved into his sweat-run features, pulled up sharply. His feet were in the inverted vee of Wallace's splayed thighs. Thus, as he thrust down into a kneel, his knees slammed into the groin of the blacksmith.

A scream of agony was forced from the injured man's throat, and he folded upward to try to ease the pain in his lower belly. Steele's right hand, still in a fist around the handle of the knife, slammed a vicious punch into the dropped jaw of

Wallace. The man's mouth snapped shut to the sound of crunching teeth—and he was sent into a writhing sprawl again.

"Steele!" Harvey Grover shrieked as both holed doors of the livery were flung open.

The Virginian looked up, and showed the two brothers the killer glint in his dark eyes and the brutal line of his mouth. Harvey was on the left and Leroy on the right, just silhouettes against the bright sunlight of the street behind them. But the leveled Colts in their hands were as starkly black on a lighter shade as their tense rigid forms.

"We heard the shootin'," Leroy said.

Steele ignored the smaller, less intelligent brother to stare contemptuously at Harvey. "You want to find out who killed your sister or not, feller?" he snarled.

"Wallace?" Harvey rasped.

The Virginian was still kneeling on the belly of the blacksmith, left hand flat on the ground beside the man's ashen face and right one holding the knife against Wallace's throat. "He's just bound to say no, I reckon," he growled, and sucked in a great gulp of air.

"I swear I didn't," Wallace whispered, and blood from split gums bubbled up over his lips. "I know it looks bad for me, but I didn't kill nobody."

The Grover brothers advanced into the stable, but this time Leroy was wrong to ape the actions of his brother.

"Watch the street!" Harvey snapped. "We don't want anyone else in here."

135

Leroy turned to do as he was told. "We gonna string him up, Harvey?" he asked excitedly.

Wallace tried to scream, but Steele pressed the knife blade against the tough skin of the black-smith's throat. The flat instead of the edge, but the touch of metal was enough to terrify Wallace into silence.

Harvey Grover halted, towering over the captive and captor. "How d'you know it was him, Mr. Steele?" he asked. "You can get up now. I got him covered."

"You can go to hell!" the Virginian rasped. "I dealt myself into this and I don't reckon to fold until it's over."

Harvey grunted, then nodded his head. "You got the right, I figure."

"You stay right where you are, Mr. Menken!" Leroy roared. "Same goes for you ladies!" He turned to grin into the livery stable. "You won't get disturbed."

"How d'you know?" his elder brother repeated.

"Because they done like I—"

"Not you, Leroy!" Harvey snapped.

"I don't know much of anything, feller," Steele answered, concentrating his narrow-eyed stare on the sweat-sheened face of Wallace. "Except what's happened to me. And that Rose Ford isn't crazy the whole time. She was rational enough when she told us a horse went missing in the night."

"Wallace stole it?" Harvey dropped into a crouch, continuing to augment the threat of the knife with his aimed gun. "To replace the one he had to destroy?"

The blacksmith was breathing rapidly, and almost choking from time to time as he gulped on his terror.

"Boyd said he owned five horses," Steele answered. "There were only four of his here this morning. And he came back to town riding the roach-backed gray."

"What you got to say about that, Noah?" Harvey demanded, thrusting the muzzle of the Colt to within a half inch of the blacksmith's right eye.

The eye screwed shut instinctively. The other one moved rapidly in its socket, swinging from Steele to Grover and back again. "I didn't kill no one!" he pleaded hoarsely. "Honest to God, I didn't."

"You weren't duck hunting last night," Steele growled.

"If I tell you ... will you promise me—"

"You ain't in no bargainin' position, Noah!" Harvey cut in.

"Just need to know," Steele said. "What happens afterwards is no concern of mine. None of this ever was."

"It don't reflect well on Abigail, Harvey!" Wallace warned. "Be in the interest of her memory to keep it secret." He gulped. "And if that don't mean nothin' to you, I can afford to—"

"Just tell it, Noah!" Harvey snapped.

The blacksmith closed both eyes, to gain whatever comfort he could from the darkness behind the lids as he confessed his crimes.

"You got nothin' to blame yourself for, Steele. Nobody has who was at the lynchin' of Emmet Ford. He killed Marty Fuller sure enough. I saw him."

"Why should we believe you, Noah?" Harvey asked.

"Let him talk!" Steele snarled.

"But it wasn't on account of money. They were in an argument about somethin' in the safe out back of the store. I came in right at the end of it. Heard the kid call Marty a string of dirty names. Then he shot him. Saw him through the doorway—with the gun in his hand. He saw me and I figured I was a goner. But he didn't take a shot at me. He just let out a sob and ran like hell out the back way.

"I went through and saw the safe open with all the money in it—and Marty stone dead on the floor."

He opened his eyes now, to show what might have been sincerity glimmering through the fear and shame. "I want you to know, it was the first real dirty thing I ever did in my life. I just grabbed them bundles of bills and hid them in a closet over at Marty's place. Wasn't time to do anythin' else, on account of folks were comin' from all over after the shot."

He screwed his eyes closed again, after seeing that his plea had drawn no response from either Steele or Grover.

Then the Virginian said: "The woman saw what you did?"

Harvey snarled, like an angered animal.

"Yeah. I turned around after closing the closet door and there she was."

"No!" Harvey groaned. And pushed the gun muzzle hard against Wallace's eyelid.

The blacksmith gasped.

"Makes sense, feller," the Virginian drawled

138

softly. "Doesn't make sense to kill him before we know the rest."

Harvey's gun hand was trembling. He controlled the movement, then abruptly came erect and turned his back on the man he had been a sliver away from killing. But he remained there, listening.

"When we got back from the lynchin', I went into Marty's store," Wallace continued, still tense from the brush with death. "The money was where I'd hid it. And your sister was there waitin' for me, Harvey. Said we oughta split it fifty-fifty."

"Did you?" Grover asked with a tremor in his voice.

"It's still over there in the closet. We made the deal and agreed to let the money stay for a while. It was as safe there as anywhere until things quieted down."

"Takin' a long time to do that," the elder Grover said softly, then raised his voice. "Keep watchin' the street, Leroy!"

The younger brother had been staring, open-mouthed, into the livery as Wallace made his confession.

"We had to act like nothin' had happened except for the killin' and the lynchin'," Wallace went on, speaking faster now, anxious to get it over and done with. "Abby takin' a shot at you was part of that, Steele. But it was as much a surprise to me as it was to you."

"It was no act, her bein' broken up about Ford gettin' killed," Harvey said morosely.

"How much money softened the blow?" Steele asked.

"Abby counted it while we were out after Ford," Wallace replied. "Fifty-five thousand. You've probably seen we don't have a bank here in Fairoaks. So folks keep their own cash."

"Abigail always wanted to be rich and get away from this town," Harvey said. "Some folks figured that was why she made up to Emmet Ford. Him being so wild. That kind get rich quick and easy sometimes."

"He paid off, for a while," Steele muttered. Then, to Wallace: "Twenty-two and a half thousand wasn't enough for you?"

The blacksmith opened his eyes and directed his fearful gaze at the broad back of Harvey Grover, aware the brooding farmer was more likely to kill him in anger than the cold-eyed dude drifter. "That was the second dirty thing I ever did in my life. It wasn't so much me wantin' the whole bundle. But I knew that if Abby ran through her share, she'd always have somethin' on me." When Harvey failed to turn toward him, Wallace returned his clouded eyes to Steele. "And, a man like you, there was always the chance he'd get her to talk—if he suspected somethin'."

Steele shook his head. "I wasn't a man like me then, feller. A man like I used to be."

"Wallace seemed to understand the cryptic comment. Then hurried on again. "You hit my horse, Steele. And he died out at the water tank. I burned him because people knew he was mine. Then I stayed out in the timber all night, worried sick about what I'd done and whether Abby would talk. Restin' some and walkin' some. Finished up close to the Ford place at dawn. Didn't intend to. Just happened that way."

The Virginian pursed his lips. "Never did make sense, you stealing a horse from Rose Ford to make up for the one that died."

"She asked me last week to bring in the geldin' for new shoes. So I just took him out of the stable. Then I went out to the sawmill to do the work there I was supposed to. And came back to town after Marvin Boyd was killed."

Steele stood up now, removing the knife from Wallace's throat and returning it to the boot sheath before he straightened fully. Harvey Grover turned to look at him in surprise.

"You buyin' that last part, Steele?" he asked tensely. "First he says he tried to kill Abigail. Then he makes out he didn't kill her."

"I didn't kill her, Harvey!" Wallace pleaded, remaining on the ground, moving only his uninjured hand to explore the crusting of blood on his jaw. "Marv, neither. I didn't know what was happenin', but I figured Steele was guilty of somethin'—the way things were in here this mornin'."

"Steele?" Harvey insisted.

The Virginian had moved away from the frightened blacksmith and the puzzled farmer. To slide the Colt Hartford from the boot on the gelding's saddle.

"I believe him, feller," he said.

"You ain't the only one that has to be sure!" Harvey growled.

Steele nodded his agreement as he moved toward the open doorway of the livery. "But I happen to be the only one who matters to me. He's all yours now."

"No, Steele!" Wallace groaned, rolling over onto his side and stretching out his arms, hands clawed as if he were trying to reach the Virginian and physically draw him back. "They'll kill me for sure if they don't believe me!"

Leroy had stepped inside to join his brother, expectant and willing to follow any instructions he was given. He already wore an expression of grim intent, as a match to that contorting Harvey's face.

Steele halted briefly on the threshold, bathed in the less intense sunlight of late afternoon. He looked from the faces of the Grovers to the trembling Wallace, and showed a brutal grin. "I believe you," he said softly.

CHAPTER ELEVEN

The doors of the grocery store were locked, back and front. But a rear window submitted noisily to a blow from the stock plate of the Colt Hartford. Then Steele swung a leg over the sill and stepped inside. It was musty in there, and overheated from being tightly enclosed for so long.

He moved from the kitchen, to a living room and then into a combined storeroom and office. As he opened a closet and lifted a burlap sheet to look at the untidily stacked pile of bills, Noah Wallace screamed. Distance subdued the sound of pain, coming as it did from diagonally across the street, as the Grover brothers showed how difficult it would be for the blacksmith to convince them he was telling the truth.

Although the kind of man Adam Steele had become was many things that were evil, he was not a thief. So he left the money precisely as he had found it, and turned to the safe backed against an opposite wall in the crowded room. The door was pushed to but not locked. It swung open easily and soundlessly on well-oiled hinges. And he heard the creak of a floorboard as somebody entered the rear of the store by the same route he had taken.

The safe was of metal construction, painted green on the outside. But the interior was unpainted and hardly tarnished at all from being closed up tight most of the time. So he positioned the door so that he could see a fuzzed and distorted reflection of the room at his back as he lifted out a stack of papers.

There were no other sounds from the kitchen or living room to mark the progress of the second intruder. Across the street, Wallace screamed again. But with less force and when the sound was curtailed, a heavy silence descended over the town. The steam-driven machines at the sawmill had been stilled while the Virginian was questioning Wallace.

Steele found what he was looking for and devoted all his attention to the distorting mirror of the safe door. He held the piece of paper in his left hand and the right canted the Colt Hartford to his shoulder. His thumb cocked the hammer.

A figure appeared in the doorway from the living room. The metal showed an image of jagged outlines—a head, body, arms and legs. Filled in with a confused non-pattern of red and white.

Hoofbeats sounded, slow-moving and far off along the trail east of Fairoaks.

The image of a grotesquely shaped arm moved. Then another. Both were foreshortened in reflection. Then the whole distorted figure moved—advancing on the back of the crouched Virginian.

Steele eased the rifle hammer to the rest, aware that the newcomer was unarmed and intent upon strangling him. Then he powered erect and whirled, swinging the rifle barrel down into the palm of the hand holding the paper.

"Steele!" Harvey Grover yelled. He was out on the street, his voice raised to full volume. "Where are you, Steele? Noah didn't do it? We're sure of that now!"

The approaching horsemen drove their mounts into a gallop.

"I'll kill you, ma'am," the Virginian warned. "Unless you stay right where you are."

"Figure he's in the grocery store, Harvey!" Leroy shouted. "Maybe after the money!"

"A crazy old lady like me?" Rose Ford asked, but came to a halt six feet away from Steele. Her arms were still out in front of her, hands clawed for a stranglehold.

"Because of the crazy part," Steele told her. "I've heard people like you are a lot stronger than . . ."

"Normal folks," she finished, and let her arms drop to her sides. She had washed the filth from her body and fixed her hair back into a severely neat bun. She wore a different dress of the same style and red and white gingham as the soiled one. She had sweated a little and there was trail dust on her face and clothing. "You discovered our secret?"

She looked and spoke like a normal person herself now. If the strange light in her green eyes could be ignored. Outside, horses clattered over the wooden bridge and skidded to a halt. The glass panel of the store's front door was shattered and the Grover brothers lunged inside. The men forming the posse shouted questions at them.

"Steele?" Harvey yelled.

"In back," the Virginian answered evenly. Then nodded. "Yes, ma'am."

The door from the store area was flung open and Harvey and Leroy entered fast and pulled up short. Other men crowded into the doorway behind them. Cutler and Sherman, Farnham and Pollock. Others who Steele recognized but did not know by name. All of these weary and travel-stained from the long hunt during the hot afternoon.

"Steele!"

"What's goin' on?"

"Hey, that's Rose Ford."

"Let me through! Outta the damn way." This from Noah Wallace, as he shoved himself through the press of curious men to reach the doorway.

Steele canted the rifle to his shoulder and glanced in that direction as the blacksmith came into view. There was a great deal more blood on his face now. And one eye was closed by two of many bruises that were humped on the crimson-run flesh. He pulled up short, his uninjured eye expressing the same degree of shock as the other men showed.

"Seems you got some more explainin' to do, mister!" Cutler said into the hard silence that had settled over the room.

Steele nodded toward the open closet where the money was still on view, and then held up the paper. "Emmet didn't kill Fuller to rob him, sheriff," he answered. "Did it because Fuller was his father."

The revelation was greeted with a burst of gasps. Then the soft-spoken words of Rose Ford brought a new silence.

"Marty couldn't marry me," she said, staring down at the floor, at a brown stain of old blood

146

showing where Fuller had died. "Men go with whores for the pleasures of the flesh. But they don't marry them. Not rich men like Marty. Wouldn't let me get rid of the baby he planted in my womb, though. Give me money so I could leave the bordello and bring up Emmet decent.

"But Emmet got wilder the older he got. Maybe on account of the way he got started. Almost killed me once, when I said somethin' bad about him and his ways. My head started to feel funny a lot after that."

The audience was swelling, with men from the timber company and with the women of Fairoaks crowding into the front of the store and entering through the broken window of the kitchen at the rear.

"That was when Marty fixed it for Emmet and me to come out here. But he couldn't do no more than see we were kept comfortable. On account he was kinda bigger and richer here than he was in San Francisco. Liked and respected. Mayor and all. It wasn't right all that should be spoiled by folks knowin' he had a son by a whore out of wedlock."

"Well, I'll be . . ." Cutler muttered. Then: "What's that paper, Steele?"

"Last will and testament," the Virginian answered. "Drawn up by a law office in San Francisco. Confirming what Mrs. Ford just said and leaving his estate to her and Emmet."

"What about the killins?" Wallace growled, rubbing his lower belly where Steele's knees had slammed into his flesh.

"Reckon Emmet found the will," Steele answered. "And took exception to Fuller wanting to keep the whole thing a secret until after he was dead."

"Marvin Boyd," Wallace insisted.

"Abigail," Harvey Grover added.

His brother nodded emphatically.

Steele looked back at Mrs. Ford and all eyes switched to the same place. The strange light in her eyes was getting brighter. And her lips were starting to tremble.

"You want to tell us about those killings, ma'am?" Steele asked softly.

"Emmet's whore came to see me," the woman on the verge of another breakdown into irrationality answered. "Somebody'd told me Emmet was dead. And Marty was dead. I don't know who ..."

"It was me, Mrs. Ford," Wallace said. "When I brought his stuff out to you yester—"

"Shut up, feller!" Steele rasped.

"I was comin' into town to find out what happened," the woman went on, and those at the rear had to lean forward to catch what she was saying. "I saw Emmet's whore and I blamed her. She got off her horse and started to talk to me. But she was wicked. The world is full of wickedness. There's little an old woman can do. But I ended her wickedness."

"Oh, my God!" Harvey gasped. "For nothin'."

"What'll we do, Harvey?" Leroy asked helplessly. "She's crazy."

"I come on into town after and I knew what I'd done," Mrs. Ford continued, not hearing the interruption. "Walked and run the whole way. Don't know what happened to the whore's horse. Saw the bartender from the saloon and another man go into the stable. Drink's wicked. So are men that call on lonely women livin' a long ways from other folks—pretendin' all they want is lemonade on a hot day. I got into the livery stable at the back. Killed one of them wicked sinners right off. The other one, he tried to tell me I'd done wrong. But I showed him."

She smiled now, and the expression gave her sweat-sheened face the look of a death mask.

"The one that was already dead had a knife. I saw it against his leg. So I pretended to be listenin' to the other one. Then I cut his throat. Real quick. I wanted to kill a lot more folks then. But I knew the town was too big for one old lady. And my head was hurtin' real bad. So I went on back home. Had to hide once, when I saw the sheriff comin'."

"Well, I'll be," the lawman said again, more astonished than before.

"Grateful to you, ma'am," Steele drawled, and pushed the last will and testament of Martin Fuller toward her. "This is yours, I reckon."

The woman took it and stared at it, unaware of what it was or why she had it. Then she looked up and around at the many faces turned toward her.

"Cooler now," she said conversationally. "But it's been another hot day, ain't it? The kind when a glass of lemonade is welcome."

"Seems like we owe you a big apology, Mr. Steele," Cutler croaked, as he and the other men in the doorway stood aside, to give the Virginian room to go between them.

"My mistake," the stranger in Fairoaks answered. "You don't owe me anything for that."

149

Most people lost interest in him as he went out of the store and across the street to get his horse from the livery, for it was the crazy Rose Ford who was the center of attention. And she was in full view of everyone as he led the gelding out onto the evening street and swung up into the saddle.

She was still locked inside the world of her own madness, talking about the heat of the day and her recipe for lemonade. So there had been no need to bind her wrists. She sat astride the horse of Leroy Grover in the shade of the oak outside the saloon. Harvey was on the ground, holding one end of a rope draped over a branch of the tree. Leroy was mounted on his brother's horse, adjusting the noose around the neck of the chattering Mrs. Ford.

The children had been cleared off the street. But their mothers watched eagerly from the windows of their houses. The excitement of the audience gathered closer to the scene of the new lynching was an almost palpable thing in the cooling air of evening.

Steele experienced no emotion as he sat the saddle in front of the open doors of the livery, gazing across the street and aware that a man was approaching him.

"It's fittin' it should end this way, mister," Sheriff Cutler said as he halted alongside the gelding and rider. "The way it started, with the people clearin' up their own trouble."

"You want me to agree with you, feller?" the Virginian asked him.

The execution was delayed and Steele was puzzled by this until he saw Menken hurrying

150

along the street from the church, hands clutching a Bible and cassock billowing out behind him.

"No, mister," the lawman answered. "I don't agree with it. It's the citizens who think it's fittin'. You ain't been in this town long, but long enough to see the folks close ranks against a common enemy."

The priest was allowed through the crowd and came to a halt beside the condemned woman.

"I have to stay and see it happen, Steele. You don't."

"Reckon I do."

"See if it affects you the same way the other hangin' did?"

"Came to town to make sure the boy got what he deserved, sheriff. Already know his mother's guilty."

"But insane," Cutler pointed out. "In a court of law, that fact could have saved her from the rope."

The Virginian nodded. "I'm waiting to see if that bothers anybody else except you, feller."

"If it doesn't?"

Menken finished his prayer and nodded to the Grovers. Harvey gripped the rope tighter. Rose Ford suddenly became aware of her situation and swung her head from side to side, staring in horror at the sea of faces surrounding her. Leroy hauled on the reins of his brother's horse and the animal walked out from under the woman.

She didn't have time to scream. Her body dropped. Harvey grunted as he took the weight of it. The branch creaked. The neck of the woman snapped. She became limp, and began to turn slowly.

"Then maybe it's not so bad that I'm the kind of man I am, feller," Steele said, as Harvey released the rope and the corpse crumpled hard to the ground.

"The kind that knows what he wants and gets it any way he can?" Cutler asked.

"Like this whole town, sheriff. And maybe the whole world. When people aren't trying to be something they're not."

"So you're leavin' a lot happier than you came, uh?"

Steele nodded as he took up the reins. Then grinned. "You never feel so bad when you know others are the same as you."

"And you're leavin' with your mouth as tight closed as the Grovers and Noah Wallace—about the money in the closet and the beatin' Noah took?"

"She's dead, Jesse!" Doc Pollock yelled across the street as he rose from examining the new corpse.

The Virginian's face was impassive again as he met the lawman's quizzical gaze. "The trouble with this town isn't mine anymore, feller," he said as he heeled the gelding forward, with the setting sun behind him. "Far as I'm concerned, that's the . . .

. . . END OF THE MATTER."

But not the end of Adam Steele. He'll be back in the next book of this series.